WANTING IT ALL

THE PUNISHMENT PIT ~ BOOK ONE

LIVIA GRANT

BLACK COLLAR PRESS

Published by Black Collar Press

Wanting it All
Punishment Pit Series - Book One
by Livia Grant

e-book ISBN: **978-1-947559-32-5**
Print ISBN: **978-1-947559-33-2.**

Cover Art by Laura Hidalgo and Spellbinding Creations

First Electronic Publish Date, August 2020

First Print Publish Date, August 2020

DEDICATION

It takes a village.

No truer words have been said when it comes to this book and series. The book you are about to read has been on a journey, starting seven years ago before I was even published. Most authors will tell you they have that one book—one series or couple—that are just special. Your baby.

This series is mine.

*While this book was published as **The Passion Series** in the past, I pulled it down three years ago to give it an overhaul. While I have lovely fans that found and love me because of this series, I've always known, or at least hoped, there is a bigger audience out there for my kinky quartet. That's where you come in.*

It took multiple editors, alpha readers, beta readers, ARC readers... you name it, to whip this series into shape. I owe so many people gratitude for helping me put a new polish on the books from Gina and Bruce back in the day, to Emily, Gaby, Katie, and Niki more recently. Then Laura came in and made covers and a trailer that made me cry. You all have helped me so much and I love you all.

And yet I know I wouldn't even have this opportunity to republish if it weren't for six of my dear author friends who went into battle with me to be able to tell this story the way I wanted to. Addison, Alta, Zoe, Maggie, and Measha — you are my tribe, and thanks for having my back. I'll go into battle with you ladies any day!!

Finally, the sixth tribe member battling with me gets the most kudos of all. My dear BFF, Jennifer Bene, has loved these characters as much, if not more, as I have from day one. In fact, it was bonding over this series (and her Thalia series) that brought Jen and I together in the first place over seven years ago. Now, I can't imagine a single day of my life without this generous, kickass, fiercely loyal, Type-A woman in it. Everyone who falls in love with Lukus is gonna have to wrestle Jen for him since she licked him years ago.

Since this is already the longest dedication in the history of dedications, I'll tack on one more mention.

This story started back in the days when a big part of me thought my dream of being a writer was just a crazy wish. I was working sixty hour work weeks and spending every free minute I had on my dream of writing, yet not once did my husband complain. He has been my biggest cheerleader from day one, taking on a ton of jobs around the house I used to do just so I could pursue my dream. Every author should be so lucky to have someone like him in their corner.

~Livia

BLURB

Everyone has a dark secret from their past... hers just forced his way back into her life.

Brianna's moment of weakness cost her everything but she's not giving up.
She'll do anything... *anything*... to convince her husband to give her a second chance.

Even if it means facing her demons and finally accepting the darkness which lies within.

The only problem is... she's not the only one with a past.

It turns out... her husband has secrets of his own.

CHAPTER ONE

MARKUS

The room was still pitch black as Markus rolled away from his wife, reaching to swat at the buzzing cell phone on his nightstand. As his brain rebooted for the day ahead, the anxiety he'd tried to press down before bed crashed in.

To say there was a lot on the line was an understatement. If things didn't go his way today, one of his oldest friends would be paying a high price.

"Too early," Brianna mumbled, burrowing closer to his warmth, flinging her arm across his bare torso.

A few minutes wouldn't make a difference—one more snooze. He wrapped the love of his life tighter in his arms, enjoying how she snuggled into his chest as her pillow.

Brianna Lambert was many things, but a morning person wasn't one of them. Still, these quiet minutes he spent holding her close each morning were some of his favorite of the day. He took a drag of her vanilla and lavender shampoo, letting the calming scent wash over him.

He had just relaxed enough to doze off when the alarm rang again. There could be no more delays.

"Don't go," she sighed as he used his Apple Watch to turn off the alarm, preparing to roll out of bed.

"Today, more than ever, I wish I could stay. But I need to get going. I'm due in court early downtown." He left off the part that he was meeting his clients, one an old college roommate, for breakfast first. The men needed to review a few things before they went into closing arguments that morning.

"I thought you tried to avoid court on Fridays," Brianna mumbled against his body.

"Yeah, well sometimes it just doesn't work out that way. This case is kinda different from my normal docket." He was hedging. Right on time, the crush of guilt sat on his chest, making it hard for him to breathe.

"Is this still the case you're doing to help some old friend?"

He'd at least told her that much.

"Yeah, but with any luck the judge will dismiss the charges today and it'll finally be over." Even as he said them, the words felt like the lie they were. A dismissal was more than a long shot, at least with Judge McKinney on the bench. She'd made it perfectly clear that she thought Lukus Mitchell was a barbarian. The thought of a submissive woman voluntarily submitting sexually to a dominant man was a foreign dynamic for the feminist judge. Their only hope was that the jury didn't feel the same.

He was just about to push out of bed when he felt Bri's hand drifting lower under the covers until she'd wrapped her slender fingers around his cock. Despite the pending stress of the day, his shaft rose to the occasion.

"Bri... I need to get up. Oh, shit... that feels amazing."

Her strokes from base to tip were erratic. She was right-handed, and pre-dawn challenged, yet still, the pressure she used as she jacked him off was perfect.

"You'd better stop unless you want to have to change the sheets today," he tried to warn her.

The tinkle of her laughter was his drug of choice.

"I have the perfect solution," she bragged mischievously just before diving headfirst under the covers.

"Bri, sweetheart, I don't have time..." But he swallowed the rest of his objection as soon as her warm, wet mouth encased the tip of his erection.

Surely, this was what it felt like to be in Heaven.

Her licks grew bolder, sucking as she used her talented tongue until he was fully erect. When Brianna removed her hand and took his cock into her mouth, he had to forcibly grab the comforter with his

LIVIA GRANT

right hand, gripping the fabric hard to avoid thrusting his hips off the bed. Despite the heavenly warmth her mouth provided, the urge to turn his devilish nature loose was strong. It took all of his willpower to let her maintain control of the leisurely pace of her loving blowjob when all he wanted to do was hold her head hard against his groin so he could roughly face-fuck her until she gagged and cried for mercy.

Get the fuck out of my head.

Memories of his sexual past had been flaring up with a concerning frequency and as always, he pushed them aside. Brianna was his do-over... the love of his life. He was determined to hold his old demons at bay because she deserved a better man than he had been. She deserved the world.

Once he'd swept unwanted memories aside, the pleasure of her bobbing head washed over him. Markus moved his hand to her silky, dark mane, stroking her softly as her tongue tickled the tip of his cock between gulps around his shaft.

"Fuck..." Still fighting his natural instincts, he warned his wife. "I know you don't really like swallowing, sweetheart. Consider yourself warned that you are about to have a mouthful if you don't—" The rest of his sentence got cut off as he let the orgasm roll through him. What might have been lost in the gentleness of the moment was more than made up for by the wave of love he felt to the depth of his core for the woman struggling to lap up every drop of

4

his hot cum. He should have felt guilty at her gagging, but her struggles only threatened to wake up his demon again.

As she kneeled up beside him, her bare breasts calling out for attention, he wanted nothing more than to stay in bed all day, making love to his wife. *If only.*

Markus reached over to pinch a tit playfully, offering, "You want me to take care of you now?"

Brianna fell back to the bed, giggling as she teased him, "Naw. I know you're already running late."

Markus chuckled, leaning down to place a kiss on the veil of dark hair covering her face. "You don't fool me. You just want to go back to sleep," he teased.

"Of course, I do," she mumbled.

"So... sleep is more important than sex. Got it."

"It is at six in the morning. Be happy I had enough energy to send you off with a smile."

"Oh, I'm happy alright." He could tell she was already sliding back to sleep. "Do you have your alarm set? You don't want to piss Tiffany off by being late again."

"Uh-ha..." she muttered, fading fast.

His phone ringing on the nightstand made them both jump. There was only one person who'd be calling at this hour today. Giving Bri a final kiss, he whispered, "I'll call you later, sweetheart. Maybe we can go out for dinner tonight."

"Okay..." she whispered, almost back to sleep.

Markus waited until he was half-way to the master bathroom before he answered on the next ring. "Hey, I'm jumping in the shower now."

"Tell me we've got this," the worried voice of one of his oldest friends said at the other end.

Pushing down his own uncertainty, he tried to sound strong. "We've already gotten the criminal case thrown out, didn't we? It's a bullshit lawsuit."

Cold water sputtered to life as he turned on the shower before walking to the sink to brush his teeth as Lukus chattered on at the other end. "I'd feel better if the judge didn't hate me so much."

Markus tried to keep his client calm. "I told you she was a hard-ass. I'm just counting on her being a fair hard-ass."

"I need this to be over. This nightmare has been hanging over my head for a fucking year now. I want it done. For life to go back to normal."

Markus chuckled. "Don't give me that. I know you and Derek have had things back to business as usual since the criminal charges were dropped."

"You know what I mean. It's not the same. I've had to..." Lukus let his voice drop off.

"What? Rein it in? Maybe that's not a bad thing," he countered.

"Fuck that. I feel sorry for the subs at the first show after this is behind me."

Markus didn't say anything, but he knew his friend spoke the truth.

Lukus closed the call. "Derek and I are about to leave here now. Meet you at the diner."

Markus's "Later," fell on deaf ears as the call had dropped.

Today was gonna be a big day. He could feel it, and he always trusted his gut on these things.

CHAPTER TWO

TIFFANY

Tiffany glanced down at her watch as her best friend came crashing into the back office of the salon they owned together. Not bad. She was only ten minutes late today.

"Morning, Brianna."

"I know. I know. I'm late for Mrs. Shriner's cut and color. Let me just throw my stuff down and I'll be ready to go."

"It's your lucky day," Tiffany replied. "She called and is running a few minutes late herself."

Brianna turned, a relieved grin on her face. "That is lucky! Now I might even have time to grab some coffee. I was running so late I had to leave home without it."

Tiffany whistled. "Wow, you slept in late enough to skip coffee. You must have been up late."

"I wish. More like up early."

Having lived with Brianna for several years,

Tiffany found that unlikely. The '*don't bullshit me*' look on her face must have conveyed her skepticism because Brianna continued.

"Markus had to get up early for a big day in court. I was a good wife and tried to send him off with a smile this morning... if you get my drift."

"Oh, I get your drift, alright. It really is true love for you two. Only Markus could entice you to get up early. You hate morning sex."

"I don't hate morning sex. I hate... shit... never mind."

"What?" Tiffany had been glancing through the appointment book but when Bri didn't answer she looked up in time to catch a look on her best friend's face she knew well.

"Oh no. Not this again." Impatient with this topic, Tiffany added, "You have to tell him the truth."

"I can't," she whined. "I love him too much. He won't understand."

"You don't know that!"

"Yes, I do. This is all my fault. I was too honest with him when we first started dating."

Tiffany laughed. "There is no such thing as too much honesty, Bri."

Kennedy, their star employee, stuck her head in the cracked door to the office. "Mrs. Shriner just got here, Bri."

"Okay, tell her I'll be right out. I just need to grab a cup of coffee first," Brianna answered.

"Got it."

Tiffany knew better than to waste time arguing with Brianna today about being more honest with her husband. They'd been through it before too many times to count. They'd go through it again as many times as they needed to until Brianna eventually plucked up the courage to talk to her husband about the darker secrets in her past.

Sticking with business, Tiff added, "We're booked almost solid today and I'm worried about walk-ins. I called Sydney and asked her to come in for a few hours this afternoon. She wasn't crazy about the idea, but I know she needs the money for her honeymoon. She's also working tomorrow all day."

"Smart! Prom season is just starting. We're gonna be busy."

"Yeah, and this way we might actually be able to get a lunch in. Let's do this!"

Several hours and many cups of coffee later, Tiffany's back was killing her. She'd been on her feet non-stop for almost five hours, working through lunch and grabbing a few bites of a cold sandwich between clients. Glancing at her best friend across the room, she could tell Brianna needed a break as much as she did.

A few minutes later, the bell ringing on the door to the shop was a welcome sound. She expected to see their employee, Sydney, but Tiffany dropped the pile of folded towels she'd been carrying when she saw who was standing in the foyer of The Beauty Box. The smug look on the man's face made her stomach churn—both anger and fear crashing in on her.

Anger won.

"What the hell are you doing here? Get out now before I call the cops!" she yelled as she stalked toward the tall man, waving her arm and pointing at the door. His expensive suit may fool others, but she knew the truth about the asshole hidden underneath.

"Tiffany, baby, you're looking as hot as ever. Although you should really lose the smock. It does nothing for showing off that curvy figure of yours."

"Cut the shit, Jake. You aren't welcome here. Get out." She felt all eyes in the salon turning her way as she was uncharacteristically rude to a patron.

"Is that any way to greet an old friend?" His devious smile highlighted his perfect, white teeth.

"We've never been friends."

"Aw, that hurts. And here I thought you'd have learned by now how important I am to a certain someone in your life." His veiled words brought her fear to the forefront, because she knew he still had the power to destroy more than one person in her life.

Grateful her best friend had gone to the back of the salon for supplies, Tiffany was desperate to get Jake Davenport to leave before he saw Bri.

"You're as delusional now as you were years ago. Bri hates you, just like I do. And lucky for her, she's not here so you can take your sorry ass out and don't bother coming back."

Jake's smile didn't fade, but when he reached up to take his sunglasses off, the chilled ice of his blue eyes was anything but friendly. Tiffany shivered as if that icy gaze could lower the temperature around him.

"That's a naughty girl, Tiffany. You shouldn't lie to me like that."

"I…"

He held his hand up, finally letting his smile slip. "Don't bother. I know Bri is here. She's in the back." He paused, nodding in that direction before letting a small smile return. "I'll wait."

"No, you won't. If you don't leave in the next thirty seconds, I'm calling the police."

He moved like a ninja, grabbing her biceps and pulling her against him so fast it took her breath away. Tiffany struggled to free herself from his grip, but Jake overpowered her to whisper against her ear. "Don't make a scene. We both know you aren't gonna call the police. If you do, I'll be forced to share a few special video tapes I've been keeping secure in my safe. You wouldn't want that to happen, would you?"

She'd expected the threat. She'd lived with it for several years now. It didn't make it any easier to keep her heart from thumping out of her chest. "You don't scare me anymore, Jake. I'm done letting you blackmail me into silence."

"We'll just have to see about that, won't we?"

Neither of them had noticed Brianna's return from the back until she was standing next to them. "Let her go, Jake. Tiffany's right. I told you last time, you're never welcome here again. I warned you then we'd call the police."

Jake turned his glare from Tiffany to Brianna. "Oh, and just what exactly are you gonna tell them, Brianna? How much you miss me and the things I do to your body? How you can't wait for me to come to town so we can resume our little tête-à-tête?"

Brianna reached out to try and make Jake release his grip on Tiffany as she berated him, "I don't miss a damn thing about you, Jake. Let her go, now!"

Jake released Tiffany so quickly she stumbled backwards, trying not to fall to the floor. When he traded his grip to Brianna, Tiffany started hitting at him.

"You have ten seconds now, or I'm calling 911!"

Jake yanked both women toward him, growling near their ears. "I'm not leaving here without Brianna. If you attempt to call the police, I promise you, I won't be the one they take in for questioning. Do you really want to bring the police down on you both and your families?"

Tiffany wanted so much to hold her ground. To tell him to fuck-off and to pick up the phone and punch those three little numbers, but familiar dread clouded her judgement. If it was just about her, she'd call in a heartbeat, but there was too much at stake for more than just her.

Brianna hesitated, probably worrying about the same things, but then she spoke up. "I'm not going anywhere with you, Jake. Not again."

Tiff wanted to reach out and wipe that wolfish grin off his face as he leaned in close to Bri. "I seem to remember you loving coming with me last time I was in town."

Sheer panic seemed to be pouring from Brianna at the mention of what they both knew was the biggest mistake of her life.

Brianna lowered her voice as she spat, "Don't you dare bring that up. It's over. You need to get it through your thick skull. I'm done with you."

"Isn't that too damn bad, because I'm not done with you by a long shot," Jake growled.

"Then we have a problem, don't we? I'm happily married. I'm not leaving here with you. Period."

"We'll see about that." Jake released Brianna as quickly as he'd snapped her into his arms. Tiffany glanced around the salon and realized they'd already gotten everyone's attention. Employees and customers alike were watching the drama playing out with interest and they needed to get him out of there.

"Jake..." she started.

"What are you gonna do, Tiffany? Willing to bet your brother's lives on this?" he taunted, and fear pierced her again.

Brianna spoke to her through gritted teeth. "It's okay, Tiff. I don't want you mixed up in my problems anymore. Let me handle this."

Tiffany rounded on her. "This isn't your problem, Bri. It's *our* problem. And you're not seriously considering going anywhere with him, are you? Not after last time!" Tiffany pleaded with her best friend.

"Of course not! I don't want to go anywhere with him, but we can't stand here in the middle of the shop arguing like this. At least if I get him outside, you can get things back to normal."

"Fuck normal. You promised me. Never again."

"I'm not gonna leave with him. I'll just step outside and talk to him and make him leave."

Even Jake laughed at that comment. "You can try, baby. But I've got money on you getting in my car with me within the next five minutes."

Tiffany didn't say it, but she was worried Jake might be right. Brianna was a smart woman in literally every aspect of her life except when Jake Davenport was involved.

Brianna started walking toward the exit, glancing over her shoulder at Tiffany as she left. She saw the same helplessness she felt to her core shining back at her from Bri's glance.

Tiffany stood frozen until they were almost out the door. "Don't do this to me!" she yelled as they walked out. Then, under her breath, she added, "Don't do this to Markus."

Tiffany ran to the door, keeping watch as Jake led Brianna toward the sports car parked in the handicap spot.

Figures the asshole would park there.

Tiff reached into the pocket of her smock to touch her cell phone, subconsciously making sure she was ready to call 911 if needed. She took up watch out the glass front door with dread. *Good, Brianna yanked free of him.* She couldn't hear what they were saying, but they were arguing. Brianna was a good foot shorter than Jake, but Tiffany almost cheered when her best friend shoved Jake hard enough that he fell back against his precious car and started heading back toward the shop.

"Thank God. I was so worried he'd haul you off once he got you outside," Tiffany gushed, relieved when Bri came back in. It wasn't until Bri went behind the counter and picked up her purse and unplugged her phone from the charger that Tiffany realized what was really happening.

Bri wouldn't look at her, but Tiffany reached out to grab her wrist, ready to tie her up to keep her at The Beauty Box. "No. I'm not letting you go. You don't have to do this. Let him try and take those tapes to the police. He talks big but he won't do it."

Bri's shoulders slumped as a tear fell down her cheek.

Tiffany pulled her closer. "What did he say? You know you can't believe anything he says..."

It was only then that Brianna held out something she'd had in her hand. Tiff reached for it and her world fell apart. She scrambled to make sense of it, to come up with a way out of the mess that was Jake Davenport — but the picture was damning.

"This proves nothing. It could have been taken years ago," she offered up hopefully.

"He has over a dozen others, Tiff. I'm the stupidest person ever. You warned me. You can tell me I told you so now."

"Dammit, Bri, I'd never do that. This doesn't change anything. You can't go with him."

"He's gonna send them to Markus, Tiff. If I don't go with him and see what he wants, I'm going to lose Markus."

"You already know what he wants, and you could lose Markus anyway. Hell, you could lose your *life*. Do I need to remind you about—"

"Stop! I don't need a reminder. It's not like I could ever forget."

"Then how can you even consider going anywhere with him?"

Bri took a deep breath before answering. "Because I love you and your brothers. And I love Markus. This is the only way to keep from hurting all of you."

"Bullshit. We need to call 911."

"Oh yeah, and say what? What has he done that the cops will care about?"

"Are you kidding me? He's—"

"I have no proof, Tiff. Nothing," Bri said, swiping at the tears on her cheeks. "The time to call 911 came and went four years ago."

"Fine. Then let's call Markus. He'll protect you."

Brianna hesitated. For a moment Tiffany thought

LIVIA GRANT

she might have gotten through to her, but with a sigh, Bri said, "I refuse to drive anywhere with him. I'll have my own car. I'll keep him in public. I have my phone with me, and I'll be back as soon as I can. He said he'll give me the photos on a hard drive if I go with him. I have to do this, for both of us, okay?"

"You know damn well he has copies. Going with him is only going to give him the chance to get more dirt on you."

"Please, Tiff... I just have to try. If I piss him off, you know he'll come after both of us. He'll go after your brothers. I can't let my shit mess with you or your family."

Tiffany knew Bri better than any other person on the planet. She recognized the stubborn glare staring back at her. Brianna had made up her mind, and she was doing it because she wanted to keep her and her brothers safe. "You're making a mistake."

"Yeah, and unfortunately, he has proof that it isn't my first time."

"Two wrongs don't make a right, Bri. I know you're trying to do the right thing, but this isn't it. Please don't do this."

For a brief second, Tiff thought she had gotten through to Bri, but then she saw that stubborn look in her friend's eye and knew she'd lost the battle.

"I can't have my screw ups ruin your life too. I'll be safe, Tiff. I promise," Bri insisted before leaving.

CHAPTER THREE

BRIANNA

amn him. Just take the next exit and drive back to the shop, Bri.

D

But as the next exit passed, the skyscrapers of the Chicago skyline only got closer.

Shit, shit, shit.

Jake had told her he'd go somewhere close. Somewhere open, and public. Of course, he'd lied. It was what he did.

"Siri—call Asshole."

Her SUV made the call to the car directly in front of her. It went to his voicemail.

"Jake, I'm done. I'm getting off at the next exit and going back to the shop. Don't follow me. Don't phone me." Brianna paused, her brain scrambling to find the right words to make her ex understand they were over, once and for all. In the end, she tried a new tactic instead of anger. "Please."

She ended the call just as she pulled into the far-right lane, preparing to exit the Eisenhower Expressway to turn around.

The ding of an incoming text message didn't surprise her.

Don't look. It doesn't matter what photos he has. It doesn't matter that he has dirt on you that will ruin your marriage. It doesn't matter.

Except... it did matter. The thought of losing Markus terrified her. It felt like she was in the biggest gamble of her life. To go anywhere with her abusive ex was marriage suicide, but to ignore his threats would put more than just herself and Markus at risk. Tiffany... her brothers. She hated that they'd been dragged into this mess right alongside her.

"Fuck..." she cursed into her empty SUV as she drove past the Oak Park Avenue exit.

The ding of another text was almost immediate. Ding... ding... ding... They were coming fast and furious.

She needed to keep her eyes on the road. Traffic was heavy, but curiosity took hold and wouldn't let go. The second she saw the X-rated photos he'd sent of her naked and tied down, her desperation spread. The worst was the angle showing the ecstasy on her face as Jake fucked her from behind.

But it was the final ding that sealed her fate. It was almost the same photo. The only difference was the addition of the Chicago Tribune newspaper Jake held above her head, a shit-eating grin on his too-handsome face.

Brianna's heart sank. She'd been too gone to notice his little photo op, but she didn't need to blow up the picture to know that she'd find the paper dated in October—six months earlier—but a full three years after she'd promised herself to her husband. It was the biggest regret of her life.

I'm gonna lose him. He'll never forgive me. How can he, since I haven't even forgiven myself?

Through her panic, she tried to think of her options. She could call 911, like Tiffany suggested. Jake had been violent with her many times in her past, but even she knew calling 911 today wouldn't do anything to help her situation.

That left only two other options. She could drive to Markus's office. It was downtown in the loop, not far from the river. He was going to court today, but maybe he'd be back by now. She could throw herself at his mercy. Come clean. Tell him everything about her sexual needs and how Jake had figured out a sick way to exploit those needs. She knew Markus loved her. He might forgive her.

But... he might not. He might think she was a sicko... a whore... a cheating, sicko, whore.

Or, she could get the compromising photos and videos from Jake, once and for all, and bring this insane mess to an end. She'd rather die than knowingly hurt Markus or her marriage.

That meant passing all of the remaining exits as she followed Jake's sports car through the early afternoon downtown traffic. She wasn't surprised when he finally ended the drive under the carport of the downtown Marriott hotel.

Brianna grabbed her purse, jumping out of her car to quickly speak to the uniformed valet attendant approaching her window. "Hi... I'm actually not staying. I just need to talk to that guy up there for a few minutes. Can you hold my car here in the car port for just five minutes?" She pointed at Jake who was handing over his keys to a different attendant.

The young employee glanced around at the busy space. "We're pretty busy. I really should..."

Bri reached into her bag and came out with her wallet. It only took a ten-dollar bill to buy her the five minutes.

"Okay, I'll move you over here out of the way for a few minutes."

"Thanks." She smiled, trying to keep her panic from showing. That only lasted until she spun to approach Jake and found him missing. In the space of a few seconds the asshole had ducked inside.

She was being played. She knew it. She was the mouse to his cat. The bait to his bite.

Time to bite back.

She stepped into the grand lobby, glancing around until she found Jake waiting for her near the bank of elevators. He'd kept his mirrored sunglasses on, his hands shoved into his tailored slacks, his tanned arms showing muscles and an expensive watch. She'd been down this path before.

Grabbing her phone, she shot off a quick text.

You got me here. We'll talk in the bar. I'm not leaving the public space.

Bri didn't wait to see if he'd follow. She turned to her right and weaved through the mostly empty tables to sit in a booth on the edge of the space.

It was an odd game of chicken. The texts started almost immediately. More threats to forward the photos to Markus.

She held her ground. She wasn't going to get behind a closed door with Jake Davenport. Not again.

She almost broke her own resolve when, after five minutes, Jake texted his contact record for Markus, proving that he had her husband's work and cell numbers. It proved he could ruin her life in the span of a few seconds.

But she stayed put, nervously glancing at the bank of windows out to the carport. As the minutes ticked by, her heart rate inched up until she saw the valet moving her SUV away, probably parking it in the hotel garage.

There goes my quick escape.

Bri suspected Jake had been waiting for her car to be removed because he started weaving his way through the lobby bar before she even lost sight of her vehicle.

"Playing hard to get, eh?" he gloated as he sat next to her on the same side of the booth.

What an idiot. I should have sat closer to the edge.

"Do not sit on this side," she ground out, trying

not to draw any attention from the few other occupants at nearby tables.

Jake took his glasses off, setting them on the table before leaning close. "I thought you'd appreciate me sitting close so no one can hear what we're talking about."

Shoving him with no effect, Bri grumbled. "We don't have anything to talk about. Just give me the pictures and videos and I'm out of here."

"Where's the fun in that?" He had the gall to wave down a passing waitress. "Hey there, babe. We'd like two Cosmos. Make 'em strong."

"No!" Brianna shouted, too loudly. Trying to temper her voice, she added, "I'll be driving soon. I don't want to drink." The server glanced back and forth between the two of them, standing awkwardly until Bri said, "Just bring me a water."

"Boy, living with Lambert sure has turned you into a bore," he goaded, grabbing a few nuts from the snack mix bowl and popping them into his mouth as soon as the waitress left them alone.

"Don't even say his name," she protested, pushing on him again to try and get him to move to the other side of the table. Instead of working, it only made Jake snake his arm behind her shoulders and yank her tight against his body.

His words against the shell of her left ear sent shivers through her body. "Don't you just love this game we're playing? It's so cute that you still try to play hard to get with me when we both know I'm gonna win every single time."

He was so damn smug, and it scared her. She hated how he'd boxed her into a corner, but even more than that, she hated that her body was starting to betray her already. It recognized what her brain was fighting.

"Knock it off, Jake. It isn't gonna work this time." Even she heard the waver in her voice, but she tried to be brave. "I don't even know why you're wasting your time on me. Surely, you can manage to get a date or two without having to harass me."

He was close enough she felt his breath on her cheek as he answered. "Believe me, it sort of pisses me off too, but let's face it. There's just something special... explosive... between us. I know you miss it as much as I do."

Brianna refused to let her mind go there. She had to be strong.

"Very funny. I don't miss your verbal and physical abuse."

"Potato, potàto. You say abuse. I call it discipline." He paused and added, "A punishment fuck," in a low growl.

She hated that her core physically constricted at his raunchy words. "I know what you're doing. It isn't going to work on me."

"We'll see about that," he said just as the waitress returned with a Cosmo and glass of water. "Just throw these on my room bill, will you, babe?"

Bri caught the annoyed look on the server's face at the term of endearment. "Sure thing, Mr. Davenport. Just let me know if there's anything else I can help with during your stay." The server hesitated like she was about to say something more before moving along.

She was surprised the woman knew his name, but as soon as she'd left them alone, Jake couldn't help but brag. "Her name is Meredith, and she's one of the reasons I always come out to see you when I'm in town. Just like every other woman I've banged since you left me, she's a complete bore in bed."

"You slept with the waitress?"

"We didn't sleep, although it was boring enough, I almost knocked off mid-fuck. Probably just like you do with vanilla Lambert every night."

"You don't know the first thing about my husband... or my marriage."

"I know he's never given you an orgasm even close to those I've given you."

Don't go there, Bri. Stay strong.

"He's also never almost put me in the hospital. What's your point?"

"My point is I know you, probably better than you know yourself. You need me, Bri. The pain... the pleasure... I can smell you, you know. Your brain may still be fighting it, but your body is already priming itself for my dominance."

She didn't deny his accusation, but she did reject it. "I'm done letting my body make stupid choices.

Now, I'll wait here while you go upstairs. You promised to give me the hard drive you have everything stored on. I'll wait here," she repeated.

Jake smiled that sexy grin that had trapped her the first night they'd met. She saw the humor in his eyes. Threatening her and those she loved was all just a fun game to him. He picked up the Cosmo and downed the strong cocktail, slamming the empty glass down with a thud just before pushing to his feet to stand at the end of the table.

Reaching into his pocket, he came out with a hotel key packet, a large 917 handwritten on the outside.

When she didn't reach for it, he threw it onto the table in front of her. "You want the hard drive you'll have to come and get it. I'll take a photo of it when I get upstairs and text it to you, just so you know I really did bring it with me. You'll have five minutes after I text the proof to you to come to my door to pick it up in person. After the five minutes, I'll start sending texts to your husband instead."

The asshole didn't even give her a chance to speak, not that it mattered. He wouldn't have listened to anything she said anyway.

It was a trap. She knew it. She'd come all this way for nothing. Once again, Jake Davenport had manipulated her into an impossible corner. If only she hadn't been stupid enough to get trapped by him last fall, she'd maybe take her chances today. Markus wouldn't have liked hearing about her sexual history, but he might have understood.

But it was moot. Once she'd had sex outside her marriage even once, Jake had won. And he knew it. The videos with threats to Tiffany and her brothers were bad enough. The photos of Bri having sex with Jake was worse.

The photo with the Chicago Tribune proving the date of her fall. That was game over.

Bri sat there, spinning her stupidity over and over until the ding of a new text felt like a knife to her heart. The asshole had the nerve to take the photo of the hard drive as part of a selfie. He'd taken off his tie and jacket. The button of his shirt collar was undone, looking casual and relaxed. Only the icy blue of his eyes betrayed the danger that was Jake Davenport.

Bri looked at her watch. It was 3:25pm. She had five minutes of happiness left before her marriage blew up spectacularly.

CHAPTER FOUR

LUKUS

"Mr. Lambert, you may present your closing statement." The hard-as-nails Judge McKinney nodded in the defense table's direction, an almost-smile on her stern face.

Lukus Mitchell held his breath as his best friend pushed to his feet next to him, buttoning the jacket of his expensive suit. At his going rate of four-hundred and fifty dollars per billable hour, and even more for court appearances, Markus could afford a closet full of designer threads.

I'm lucky he's giving me a family discount.

Fuck, he wanted this fiasco to be over. They were getting close to the finish line, he just hoped the outcome was worth waiting for. As Markus started his prepared closing statement, Lukus watched the twelve-person jury, looking for any hint of what the group of seven men and five women were thinking after listening to a full day of testimony.

"Ladies and gentlemen of the jury, I want to thank you for your dedication today. I've noticed all of you listening intently, often taking notes. I appreciate that despite the salacious nature of this case, you've listened carefully to the plaintiff's attorney laying out the details of the ridiculous civil lawsuit being brought against my two clients, Lukus Mitchell and Derek Parker.

"As you learned during my defense arguments, Ms. Tarkin and Ms. Kristoff first attempted to bring criminal sexual assault charges against my clients, but the criminal charges were dismissed by the Cook County District Attorney's Office almost immediately when the DA acknowledged that the contract the plaintiffs signed when they willingly joined The Punishment Pit club outlined the exact scenario the ladies sitting to my right later objected to.

"As you heard from the three material witnesses I called to the stand earlier today, not only were the physical punishments provided by my clients within the guidelines of the membership contract, they were identical to scenes that the plaintiffs witnessed no less than four times on previous documented visits to The Punishment Pit. To pretend they were not aware of the physical nature of the stage shows is utterly ridiculous.

"Furthermore, despite being within their rights to proceed during the show in question, my clients stopped the punishment scene in question immediately when Ms. Tarkin called out the club safeword, *red*. That she chose to delay in utilizing the club safeword until ten minutes of the scene had passed is not the responsibility of my clients, who were acting in good faith.

"Finally, and most importantly, I am counting on each of you to recognize that my clients have done nothing but cooperate with the plaintiffs, offering to refund their final month's membership fees. Mr. Parker and Mr. Mitchell each took the stand today to answer questions from the plaintiffs' attorneys, and while you may or may not personally agree with the sexual activities that transpire at the club in question, I'm counting on your fairness to recognize that nothing that transpires at the property is illegal. In fact, my clients take great pride in providing a safe environment for those who share their BDSM lifestyle to congregate and play without fear of judgement. Something that I'm certain you have noticed the women refused to do themselves. By refusing to take the stand and answer my questions under oath here today, I am requesting that you find in my client's favor, dismissing all charges in this civil lawsuit. Furthermore, I ask you to find the plaintiffs responsible for Mr. Mitchell and Mr. Parker's legal fees. Thank you."

Lukus finally exhaled as Markus took his seat next to him at the defense table. If the small curl at the corner of his friend's mouth was any indicator, he'd say things had gone well today, but he didn't know jack shit about lawsuits. That they were even sitting in the courtroom pissed him off. This bogus case should have never been filed.

Markus leaned closer just as Judge McKinney started giving final directions to the jury. "I never dreamed we'd be able to get all the way to closing arguments today, but that went well, regardless. By not taking the stand themselves, the ladies have really made this a slam dunk."

Lukus would believe that when he heard their verdict himself.

He had to keep his voice down as he whispered, "Why the hell would they go to all this trouble and then not testify themselves?"

"Who the fuck knows. I could have called them myself since it is a civil lawsuit. It's a bit of a gamble, but I think the fact that they didn't testify is gonna put the nail in their case's coffin," Markus whispered back.

Lukus didn't say it, but he was ecstatic that Markus hadn't called the bitches to the stand, if only because it meant maybe putting this bullshit case behind them... finally. The scene in question had been just short of a year ago. They'd had the threat of the lawsuit hanging over their heads for long enough. Lukus just wanted it over.

It only took five more minutes before the bailiff led the jury out of the jury box, through the side door and into the bowels of the downtown courthouse. It was already early afternoon, so the chances of this being over today were slim and he knew it.

"Come on, I'll buy you guys a coffee," Markus offered.

"I need something stronger," Derek deadpanned.

Lukus agreed. "I saw a pub across the street. The first round's on me."

Markus chuckled. "Fine, but we need to stay close. I have hopes they'll come back fast."

The men were headed toward the exit, avoiding the bitches who brought them there, when Lukus asked, "Is fast good or bad?"

Markus shrugged. "Honestly... it could go either way. Let's face it. The general public doesn't get the nuances of the BDSM lifestyle. I laid it out for them as best I could, but there could always be a hard-ass in the bunch that objects to the lifestyle enough that they'll dig in."

"Fucking great."

The men had just ordered a second round of beers at the Maxwell Street Pub when the ding of an incoming text lit up Markus's phone sitting on the table. Lukus watched as his friend and attorney started checking his text messages.

Markus let out a low whistle. "That was even

faster than I could have hoped. The jury is back already."

Lukus felt a pressure on his chest, and he knew it was stress related. He'd been waiting a year to have this shit behind him. Now that he was within minutes of finding out if he was going to have to close down his club or not, he suddenly worried he might have been pushing to go too fast.

"Come on, everything's gonna be okay," Markus said as he waved at their server to bring their check.

"Promise?" Lukus asked, not really joking. "Did we push too fast?"

"Don't borrow trouble. We'll find out in a few minutes."

"Easy for you to say," Lukus snapped back. "I'm the one who'll lose my dream club if I end up having to pay out the million bucks. Not only will I need to sell to come up with the payout, but once we get successfully sued, it will prove the contract isn't gonna protect us from jack shit going forward."

"We've been through this. It's way too late to change course. Chug your beer and let's go," Markus demanded.

Lukus chuckled. "Trying to Dom the Master's Master?" he asked, taking the last lukewarm swig of beer.

"If that's what it takes, sure. Wouldn't be the first time," Markus said with a grin.

"The hell you say."

The good-natured banter of friends was exactly

what Lukus needed to keep calm as they settled up and walked back to the courthouse. It took ten minutes to make it through the lobby security and x-ray machine. Lukus felt naked having left his shoulder-holster and Glock back at his loft above the club. Courtesy of his other business, Titan Security, he had a concealed carry permit for the state and city, but he hadn't wanted to deal with trying to get a loaded pistol through security in a state courthouse.

The judge looked mildly annoyed when the men arrived back in the courtroom. The plaintiffs were already there along with the handful of spectators in the viewing area. Within a minute of taking their seats, the bailiff came in, holding the door for the jury to file into the box.

Derek elbowed him, his friend's way of saying 'good luck' as the judge started talking to the jury. Lukus tried to pay attention, this was important, but his brain kept racing, replaying the scene that landed them here over and over. No matter how many times he relived it, he could never find anything he'd done wrong.

"Ladies and gentlemen of the jury, have you reached your verdict in this case?" The judge seemed as ready to get her Friday docket finished as Lukus was.

What looked to be the oldest man sitting on the end stood to address the court. "We have, your honor."

"Bailiff... please." She nodded from the bench.

The uniformed court bailiff walked to the jury box and took the piece of paper held out by the jury foreman before carrying it to the judge.

The hard-as-nails judge took a minute to review the piece of paper before raising her gaze in their direction. When Markus pushed to his feet, Lukus and Derek followed his example.

The pregnant pause seemed to go on forever before Judge McKinney finally spoke. "In the case of Tarkin and Kristoff versus Mitchell and Parker, the jury has found in the favor of the defendants. The note from the jury indicates that they believe the contract in place and the defendants' actions on the night in question prevent them from finding in favor of the plaintiffs."

Judge McKinney looked up at the jury, verbally polling them. "Jury members, please demonstrate by a show of hands if this is your unanimous decision."

Twelve hands raised almost immediately.

Looks like they want to get the hell out of here too.

"Very well. We will enter a verdict in favor of the defendants in this case. The jury has also indicated that the plaintiffs are to be responsible for the legal costs for the defendants."

For the first time, the two women who had sat stoically at the table opposite them grumbled to their lawyer loud enough that Lukus wanted to cheer.

"Thank you for your service, members of this jury. Court is dismissed."

Lukus felt like whooping out a cheer, and Derek

slapped him on his back so hard he lurched forward. Both men turned to their friend, who was now grinning.

"See, I told you not to worry."

"You never said that. You said don't borrow trouble."

"Whatever. All I know is I wish I could be at the club tonight to see you two unleashed for the first time in almost a year."

He let a low groan loose, looking forward to his evening already.

Grabbing their briefcases, Lukus took a deep breath and made an invitation he hoped his friend would take him up on. "Now that the case is over, let me take you, Derek, and Rachel out for a steak dinner tonight. You can invite that wife of yours." Lukus paused, feeling unusually vulnerable by adding, "Don't you think it's time I finally meet her?"

A cloud of something Lukus didn't want to examine too closely crossed his friend's expression. For the hundredth time over the last four years, he tried not to feel hurt that there was a whole part of his best friend's life he'd been cut out of. It was total bullshit, to be honest.

Markus waffled. "I don't think we can make it. We already had dinner plans for tonight." His friend must have picked up on Lukus's disappointment because he added, "Let me see what I can do about getting us together in a few weeks."

But he'd said that before and a few weeks turned

to months and then years. As much as he wanted to get to the bottom of the problem, standing in the courtroom just a few feet away from the bitches who'd sued them chewing their lawyer's ass out wasn't the place or the time.

As soon as they stepped out of the courtroom, all three men turned on their cell phones as they walked to the elevators. Just before the doors opened, a long string of text messages started pelting Lukus's phone from one of his senior security technicians.

One after another the messages got more urgent.

"There a problem?" Derek asked.

"I'm not really sure. Maybe," Lukus answered truthfully.

The ding of a voicemail arrived just as they exited the elevator in the marble lobby of the courthouse. Lukus listened to the message with dread, keeping an eye on Derek and Markus as they said their goodbyes.

Well fuck. What the hell do I do with this?

Indecision hit hard. He needed to make a split-second judgement that could have lasting implications for his best friend. The very man who'd just pulled his own ass out of the fire.

Markus turned, putting his hand out for a shake just as Lukus put his cell back into his pocket. The men shook hands, but when Markus started to pull back, Lukus held on tight.

His friend knew him well. Their eyes met as

Lukus pulled him closer to talk softer to prevent being overheard.

When no words came out, Markus prompted him, "What's wrong?"

"I'm honestly not sure if you want to know."

CHAPTER FIVE

The numbers 9-1-7 would forever be burned in her memory. Against every instinct in her body, and almost on autopilot, Brianna had taken the elevator up to the ninth floor, pushing out of the crowd at the very last second. She'd sat in an uncomfortable chair near the elevator bank for almost ten minutes, trying to pluck up the nerve to just leave. She was counting on the fact that he was bluffing and hadn't already texted Markus.

As scared to death as she was about the things Jake Davenport might do to her if he got her behind closed doors, she had come to the conclusion that losing Markus would be a hundred times worse.

Her husband was everything Jake was not. Kind. Gentle. Funny. Loving. She should be relieved to have a man like him in her life after the trauma she'd suffered at the hands of her ex. And she was. And that was why she'd pushed to her feet to stand outside of room 917.

Just one more time. She'd risk getting sucked in just one more time. She'd come too far now to turn back. She wasn't leaving without the hard drive. Last time she'd been vulnerable, weak. She was stronger this time.

It was eerie that she'd just made her decision to knock when Jake swung open the door. He'd taken his shirt off and changed to a pair of perfectly fit, worn jeans. Bri'd be lying if she didn't admit that her core clenched, recognizing the effect the asshole still had on her. If only she could focus on the bad, because there was more than enough of that.

Unfortunately, her body remembered the amazing ecstasy he'd pushed her to as well. It seemed an impossible task to separate the two in her mind.

They stood in a stare down for several long seconds before she found her voice. "I'm not coming in. Hand me the hard drive."

He had the audacity to grin as he let his free hand roam across his muscular chest suggestively. "You want it, you'll come and get it."

When she stood frozen, the jerk stepped back letting the door slam closed with a loud thud. Furious, Brianna stepped forward to start pounding on the door. "You asshole! Open the door and just give me what I came for so I can leave."

The door swung open so fast, it caught her off-guard. She'd been prepared for him to make her beg, since he loved that so much. Instead, he grabbed her wrist before she could step away from the door. Jake yanked her toward him so hard it felt like he'd pulled her shoulder out of socket. Fight or flight instincts kicked in as Bri heard the door slam closed again, this time trapping her inside. Pent-up angst fueled by adrenalin helped her kick and flail, connecting her foot with his shin and her heavy purse with his shoulder.

"Don't fucking touch me!" she cried, managing to stumble far enough away that he lost his grip. Bri scrambled to the right, putting a love seat between them.

Instead of angering him, the asshole had the nerve to smile. "God, I love a good chase."

Brianna knew he told the truth. He'd proven it to her many times in the past. "You aren't gonna win this one, Jake. We're done." She took her phone out of her bag, never taking her eyes off him. "If you touch me, I'll call 911."

"Oh, and say what exactly? I'm disappointed in you, sub. It looks like all of that careful training I did with you has been going to waste with vanilla Lambert."

"I'm not your sub. I never was."

"Oh, I beg to differ, slut. You used to crawl on your hands and knees, begging me to fuck you harder." Jake took a few steps closer as he threatened her with vile memories.

"The only begging I remember was for you to honor my safeword. I wasn't a sub. I was your punching bag."

"Still harping on that? When are you gonna learn? I know your body better than you do, Bri. For instance, I know your panties are dripping right now. The skin on your ass is actually tingling in anticipation of the whipping you desperately need. We both know I'm the only man on the planet that can make you come without even touching your fucking pussy. Don't even try to deny it."

As much as she hated his words, he was right—she couldn't deny them. Every hated word was true.

"It's irrelevant. We're done. Give me what I came for and I'll leave." She moved to the end of the love seat, keeping as much distance as possible between them.

Unbothered by her defensive stance, Jake walked to the in-room refrigerator and pulled out a cold bottle of beer, twisting off the top and taking a long drag as if he hadn't a care in the world.

"Stop wasting time. I need to leave. I have appointments this afternoon."

Jake's glare returned to her, suddenly more serious. "You know, you wouldn't have to work if you were still with me. It's bad enough Lambert can't even take care of you properly in the sack, but making you help financially is stupid."

Bri scoffed. "You never did give a shit about what made me happy. If you had, you'd know that owning my own business has always been my dream. Markus helped make that dream possible."

"Whatever. If it helps you feel better about playing house out in the suburbs, I guess I don't give a shit."

"And how would that be any different than before? You never gave a shit about anything but yourself."

The smile that didn't quite reach his eyes was back. It was her warning that she was pushing him to the edge, and she knew first-hand what happened when he crashed over that cliff. "That's where you're wrong, Bri. There is one thing about you I find myself missing very much."

She didn't ask what because she knew she didn't want the answer. Instead, she reminded him why she was there. "Just give me the hard drive, Jake."

After several long seconds, he turned and walked to the desk against the far wall, pulling what looked like a hard drive from his briefcase. As he walked back toward her, she had to shift to keep the sofa between them.

"Just throw it on the cushion. I'll grab it and get out of here."

For a second she thought he was going to try to walk around to her. No one was more surprised than she was when he complied, throwing the hard drive to the cushion. Bri didn't take her eyes off Jake as she reached down, blindly feeling around until she brushed the small box, lifting it and placing it in her big bag.

Sweet relief.

She'd gotten what she came for. Until that moment she hadn't realized how low her expectations had been for her chances of success. Now, the only thing standing between her and her escape were the photos on his phone. He probably thought she was stupid enough to overlook the fact that he had copies there.

"Now your phone. Hand it over."

He grinned. "That wasn't part of the deal. I told you you'd get the drive."

"You told me you'd give me all of the pictures and videos. That includes your phone." When he just stood with his smug-ass smile, Bri yelled, "Now!"

His smile evaporated, replaced with the dangerous anger of her nightmares. She'd suspected she wouldn't escape today without seeing that side of her ex.

"Careful, my pet. I've played along today, but you forget your place."

"The only place I have in your life is in your rearview mirror. We're done, Jake. Now, give me your phone so I can leave."

"You want my phone." It was a statement, not a question. So, she didn't answer.

Even Bri was surprised when he reached into the back pocket of his jeans and came out with his iPhone. It was so unlike him to give in so easy. Still, when he held out his arm, Bri reached over the back of the loveseat, careful to keep the furniture between them, as she grabbed his cell.

She'd expected him to try to grab her arm. She hadn't expected him to launch himself over the loveseat, stepping on the cushion and vaulting into her body. The velocity of his tackle knocked them both backwards, crashing her to the carpeted floor so hard it knocked the wind out of her.

In the span of two seconds she'd lost her advantage completely. She fought to get free with every ounce of her energy, but he was too heavy as he used his strength to wrestle her flailing arms and legs into submission.

When she could catch her breath, she gritted out, "Get the fuck off me!"

The bastard had the nerve to laugh.

Bri fought like a hellcat, desperate to free herself, but with each passing second, her chances of leaving the room unscathed were plummeting. She knew first-hand what the man was capable of and that knowledge sent a full-body shiver rattling through her trapped body.

He was too strong. Too big. Too evil.

He pinned her wrists above her head, keeping her lower body trapped under the weight of his body. Jake had the audacity to lean over to lick a path down her neck to her shoulder as if he were marking his territory.

"Stop!" Bri rallied her strength for a final push for freedom, bringing her leg up to try and knee him, but it was only enough to graze the erection she felt poking her from behind his jeans. Still, Jake's grunt told her she'd been partially successful.

"You bitch, you'll pay for that."

Not if I can get the fuck out of here I won't.

She kept fighting, twisting, trying to throw him off her, but the struggle only lasted a minute more before Bri had to acknowledge the truth. He had her trapped.

She needed a new plan, and she wasn't above begging. "Please, Jake. Don't do this. Surely you can have anyone you want in your bed. Why me? Just let me go... please."

"Your begging is music to my ears," he ground out against her cheek, nipping her earlobe hard enough he might have left teeth marks.

It took a second to realize the reason he'd started contorting while holding her down was to pull a previously unseen length of rope from the back pocket of his jeans. They were both out of breath from the wrestling match by the time he had her wrists tied tightly together.

As soon as he pushed off her body, she rolled the opposite direction, using her tied hands to help push to her feet. Desperate to get out into the hallway where she could scream for help, she left her bag on the floor. She only made it two steps before he tackled her again, this time from behind. The carpet burn on her knees would surely leave a mark. She wished she'd worn slacks to the salon today instead of a dress.

Bri kicked, scrambling forward on her hands and knees just a few feet before she felt his hands on both her ankles. His hard yank had her body flopping back to the carpet with a thud. She kicked, making it hard, but not impossible, for him to get her feet tied together.

This was bad. Really bad.

It was a small consolation that Jake was breathing heavy, like he'd just finished a workout. When he pushed to his feet, leaving her on the floor, she started inching her way across the carpet toward the door, doing her best to ignore the animalistic need gnawing at her core.

"Help! Someone!" she screamed at the top of her lungs, praying another guest or housekeeper was passing by the room.

She was only a few feet from the door when the first line of fire lit up her ass. The heat licked deeper than just her skin as the bite of pain nipped at that part of herself she kept tightly locked up.

"That's my girl. I knew she was still inside there somewhere."

That was exactly what Brianna was afraid of.

"Stop! You can't do this to me!"

"Oh, slut, I disagree. Not only *can* I whip this body of yours into a frenzy—I know you want it."

"Fuck you, Jake! This will be rape!"

"Such a nasty word for something as explosive as what we have together." The next line of fire fell an inch lower across her ass. Her thin dress and panties did absolutely nothing to protect her from the assault. "Aren't you glad I remembered to throw my thickest dragon tail in my carryon? I remember it used to make you sing better than almost any other implement in my arsenal, well except maybe the cane."

Her howl of pain was anything but melodic. She just prayed someone would hear her and call security. The next strike of the leather was the hardest yet. It had been so long... yet, God help her, the next thought that popped into her brain was how much she'd missed this.

There's something wrong with me. I hate that I need this.

Jake's punishment paused, giving Brianna enough time to renew her caterpillar crawl across the carpet toward the door. Only six more feet.

Above her, she heard the unmistakable sound of one of Jake's oldest tortures. She pushed to her knees, wiggling toward the door, but he was too fast. She threw her head left and right, but the two-inch wide, six-inch-long strip of electrical tape was slapped across her mouth from behind. He'd caught a chunk of her long, dark hair under the tape.

His lips were once again against her ear. "As much as I love hearing you scream, we can't have anyone hearing how much fun we're having now, can we?"

His hands found the hem of her dress, pulling it easily over her head. She grabbed onto the fabric, trying to slow him down, but the tearing sound scared her. They were the only clothes she'd have when she left, that was, assuming she didn't die in room 917. This wasn't the first time she'd feared for her life with him, though.

Once she was down to her panties, bra, and shoes, Jake scooped her up and carried her back to the nearby sitting area. His face was just a few inches away, forcing her to slam her eyes closed. She couldn't bear seeing the sadistic glee plastered all over his face.

The deeper she got into the room, the farther the panic pulled her down. What a fool she'd been to think she could erase her biggest mistake by making an even bigger one today. She forced herself to focus on the memory of her handsome husband. If only she'd driven to Markus's office, she'd be there right now. She could have come clean. She might have still lost him, but at least she'd have avoided making things even worse.

Jake dumped her to her feet behind a heavy armchair before shoving her upper body hard enough that she fell forward, her face crashing into the seat cushion. She'd been down this road more times than she could count with Jake, so she was ready for him the second he undid the rope tying her ankles together.

Her kick connected with his shin, but only drew a chuckle from her captor as he pulled her left leg wide to the outside of the chair, tying her ankle to the wooden leg. The chair was wide, so her right ankle secured to the other leg left her spread open, at Jake's mercy.

The sound of tearing fabric came next as she felt the room's air-conditioning on her bared pussy. She grumbled behind the tape, unable to vocalize her anger at his ruining her panties, realizing that was the least of her worries.

Bri steeled herself for the pain she knew was coming. If dread and fury were her only emotions, she might have been able to lie to herself, but the spike in her pulse betrayed that a big part of her was exhilarated for what was ahead. Her heart hurt as she admitted to herself how much she'd missed it. Not Jake, but his dominance. The excitement of the chase. The submission of being caught.

Unable to see with her face in the chair, her first clue of the coming pain was the swish of the leather just before it connected with her now naked ass. She jolted hard enough that the chair wobbled. The next strike fell lower, near the bottom of her curvy ass.

The loud groan filling the room was part pain... part something else she desperately wanted to ignore.

Thwack. Thwack. Thwack.

Three fast and furious lines of heat took her

breath away. She wiggled her ass the few centimeters that the give in the ropes allowed, but it brought no relief. It helped to focus on the pain because she knew she deserved that for being stupid enough to trust Jake enough to find herself here... again.

When he moved his strikes lower to her thighs, tears filled her eyes. She fought off a sob, mainly because she knew Jake got off on being able to make her cry.

Hard. Soft. Fast. Slow. Jake played her body perfectly... or more accurately, disastrously. The red welts on her bottom weren't the only fire in room. Her pussy had started to constrict involuntarily, preparing for the coming tsunami.

Finally resigning herself to what was happening, Bri just wanted to get it over with. Unfortunately, that would be too easy. He'd always been a patient torturer, dragging out the pain... and pleasure... until he got what he wanted.

And that was usually making her beg to be fucked.

His palms were cool against the globes of her ass. His touch was deceivingly gentle, massaging as he broke the silence.

"Christ, I've missed you, Bri. I can't find anyone who marks this beautifully. Who moans so perfectly —part pain, part pleasure." His fingers slipped into the cleft of her pussy, grazing just lightly enough to bring a zing of pleasure. "No one comes close to being able to take what I need to dish out."

She hated herself for wiggling against his fingers, desperate for more pressure. A little friction was all she needed. But then his fingers moved higher, taking her copious wetness with them as they strayed higher... and...

NO!

His wet finger pressed against the pucker of her anus. Adrenalin kicked in as she pushed her torso up off the cushion, flailing to escape. Anal had always been off-limits. It was the one and only line she'd laid down that Jake had ever respected. Until he thrust a digit inside her ass, she had naively never considered that he would break yet another promise today.

She hated the tape across her mouth. She grunted and groaned as she thrashed wildly, displaying her fury at his continued exploration in her forbidden place. One digit turned to two as his other hand pressed between her shoulder blades, forcing her face back into the cushion. God, she wished he'd just go back to whipping her. She'd take the pain any day over the confusing arousal and dirtiness his fingers were strumming instead.

"So fucking tight. I'm curious, Bri. Have you given this hole to Lambert yet or have you been saving it for me?"

If he took the tape off, she'd have told him to fuck off, but since that would only egg him on, she grunted instead.

The slap of his palm on her heated bottom surprised her, reigniting the pain left by the tawse just as he started finger fucking her virgin hole. She was unprepared for the foreign pressure that felt better than she wanted to admit.

And then a second later, he was gone. The only sound in the room was her own gasping breaths as she fought to get enough air in through her running nose. That was until she heard the unmistakable flick of Jake's leather belt being pulled out of the loops of his jeans.

She almost came from the snap of the leather tip exiting his pants alone, and the fucker's chuckle at her expense proved he knew it.

"See how nice I am? I know you'd never ask me for it, but you've missed my belt."

Bri would rather cut her right arm off than admit he was right—but he was. The second the worn strip of leather laid across the heated skin of her ass, something inside her just clicked into place. It was as if she'd been walking around with a piece of herself missing, and the belt magically made her whole.

How she wanted to hate it—to feel only the pain the leather brought, but with each loud crack the pain burned deeper, touching that magical place she liked to call her *happy place*. Her orgasm was close, just out of reach. If only he'd deliver the punishment lashes a bit faster... a tad harder. He edged her for what felt like an eternity but was probably only minutes.

Bri pushed down her panic as she realized he was surely leaving bruises and welts that wouldn't fade nearly fast enough. Just thinking about how she was going to hide the evidence of the whipping helped to douse her high. As a masochist, her body craved what Jake was delivering, but her brain still rejected it. She fought to keep from coming.

Fought and failed.

Her scream behind the tape was guttural as Jake's hard cock pierced her pussy, balls deep in one thrust. He bottomed out, his fingers digging into her hips, as he yanked himself in and out at a brutal pace. The slapping of their bodies crashing together was only drowned out by the grunts of their shared exertion.

The pain as his long shaft crashed against her cervix finally succeeded at driving her to her happy place—the elusive orgasmic high she only achieved through pain. Stars blurred her vision as her core contracted, her heart pounding faster than his thrusts.

"Christ, I've missed your cunt's tight squeeze as you come." He started slapping her burning ass cheek. "Fucking come again... I know Vanilla doesn't have a clue how to make you shatter like I do."

It was impossible to stave off his raunchy order. His ramming erection partnered with the blistering spanking pelting her already striped bottom was her kryptonite, and Jake knew it. Brianna fought to hold onto her vision of Markus, but she eventually fell into an orgasmic trance where she let wave after wave of pleasure crash over her, chasing away everything but her sexual need.

LIVIA GRANT

Jake fucked her like a machine. The pace was brutal, and his staying power, remarkable. She'd just started to come down from her string of bliss when he finally pulled out, leaving her heaving to catch her breath, face down into the cushion.

Right on time, crushing regret and shame for allowing this to happen was just settling in when Jake proved once again that he was evil incarnate. Of all of the horrendous things he'd done to her over the years, he just couldn't stop trying to one-up himself.

"See how nice I am? I'm gonna use lube for your first anal fuck. I've been waiting to bugger this tight pucker of yours since I saw you last fall."

Brianna lost it. She flailed, fighting like a madwoman to get free of the ropes. She grunted and screamed, but the damn tape stole her objections, leaving her abuser to chuckle at her expense.

Wetness dribbled between her butt cheeks. She struggled hard enough that the chair rocked back and forth, but it was too heavy for her to get away from the probing fingers scissoring in her untested hole.

Despite her technically being raped already, it wasn't until she felt the tip of Jake's cock pressing against her tight ring that she felt the true weight of his violation. Up until now he'd only done to her what he'd done hundreds of times in the past when she'd been stupid enough to allow him in her life. But now—if he pressed forward, knowing she would never consent to this invasion—it was sexual assault in its rawest form.

His cock stabbed forward in a brutal thrust that violated her untried hole. The fucker plunged his hand into her long, knotted hair, yanking her upper body up far enough that he could clamp his left hand across her taped mouth.

Forcing her back to arch until it hurt, Jake grunted against her ear as he filled her ass again. "You're even tighter than I'd dreamed, but we can't have you making so much noise. I'd hate to have our fun interrupted by a nosy housekeeper."

His third thrust hurt so bad she couldn't hold back her sobs any longer. Unlike the pain of the tawse and belt that she'd mastered the skill of converting to almost heavenly pleasure, this new agony only brought ugly fury.

I didn't think he could possibly hurt me more than he has in the past. Shit, I was wrong.

The silent voice in her brain broke through the veil of pain to laugh at her. She deserved this torment for needing the dominance Jake delivered. Markus's gentle loving should be more than enough to satisfy her, but no. Her body desperately wanted to have it all, and well... this was the price she would have to pay for her deviant sexual urges.

Suffering was all she deserved, yet when Jake lowered his left hand from across her taped mouth, lower to her spread pussy, the white light of ecstasy exploded from out of the blue. Jake's hard pinch to her swollen clit detonated the best kind of agony.

His thrusts kept a fast beat until he delivered a

raunchy rant. "That's my slut. Your ass is so fucking tight, you're squeezing every drop of jizz out of my cock. You'll be remembering me for days as my cum keeps dribbling out of you."

Her back and scalp hurt. Her pussy throbbed with spent pleasure. Her clit pulsed with damning need, while her back passage felt raw by the time Jake's own orgasm finally erupted. Bri felt his spunk branding her virgin hole as he shouted out, "Brianna!"

How odd that his use of her name felt like the worst kind of violation as they each panted to take in enough oxygen to slow their breathing. Even as his cock started to deflate, her bottom hole felt weirdly full.

As much as she hated the idea of facing her tormentor again, she was relieved when he pulled out of her body. The wetness he'd left behind started to dribble down leaving a sticky streak across her skin.

A new anger flared when she heard the water turn on in the nearby bathroom. The asshole had left her tied down in the uncomfortable position while he showered. That was bad enough, but the worst was all that she had to keep her company were her regrets.

The sound of her cell phone ringing inside her bag not far away reminded her that as bad as things were, they were going to get worse. It was Markus's ring. Shame flared as she was forced to let the call from the love of her life roll to voicemail because she was tied down naked in another man's hotel room. Hot tears spilled into the chair cushion below her as she wallowed in remorse for not being across town in his office instead.

I made the worst possible choices today... again.

By the time Jake joined her fifteen minutes later, she was ready to jump out of her punished skin.

She was grateful for his silence as he worked at freeing her from the ropes. There was nothing he could say that could possibly make her feel better, and many that would make things even worse. When she got her first glimpse of him after she pushed upright from the face-plant in the cushion, she was comforted to see he'd already dressed.

When he finished removing the tape from her mouth and the bonds she found that, despite finally being free of the restrictive ropes, her legs had lost all feeling from being in her compromising position for so long. Masquerading as a gentleman, Jake scooped her up in his muscular arms and carried her to the bed, gently laying her well-used body down.

Bri wanted to hate him—to remember how awful he was and how he'd violated her body in so many ways today. Focusing on that would be easier than realizing how satiated she felt. Her brain fought the fear of losing her marriage, while the rest of her body relaxed into the unique afterglow only forced submission could produce.

Unfortunately, as he often did before his departure, Jake gave her a small glimpse of the man she'd been duped by so many times in the past. He leaned over her, wiping at her tears that continued to fall. Jake brushed her sex-mussed dark hair away from her face as he leaned in to give her a deceptively soft kiss.

The touch to her lips ignited her anger as he tried to intensify it. Bri turned her head, forcing his lips to land on her neck instead. Unwilling to lose his control over her body, Jake locked her head in a vise, forcing her lips against his in a violent assault. She resisted until his tongue pierced her mouth as urgently as his cock had invaded her body before.

The savage kiss lasted until she finally nipped at his invading tongue with her teeth to make him stop. Still, after pulling out of the kiss, Jake stayed close. Brianna slammed her eyes closed to avoid looking into his victorious eyes. She prayed he would just leave her to lick her wounds in peace.

"Open your eyes, Brianna," he whispered, deceptively soft.

She waited as long as she could in the silence, but realized he wasn't going to leave until she obeyed. When she finally opened her eyes, the emotion in Jake's deep blue eyes confused her. She'd expected him to gloat over the conquering of her body, but instead, the odd emotion shining in his eyes looked more like tenderness. "I really have missed you, Bri. You have to see how great we are together. I unfortunately need to head out to meet some clients, but I'll be waiting for your call when you finally get tired of playing house out in the suburbs with Vanilla. Don't wait too long to come to your senses, baby. I don't know how much longer I'll be able to resist picking up the phone to enlighten him myself."

Terror gripped her, knowing Jake wouldn't hesitate to blow up her life if the fancy struck him.

"Why the hell do you even care if I'm married? You suck at relationships, Jake."

"Maybe, but times change. I've had enough time away from you to realize just how perfect we are together. And if you'd be honest with yourself for one minute, you'd see that too." He looked so damn confident. He actually believed the bullshit he was shoveling.

"You're fucking crazy. The only thing we do well is sex. It's true, you may know how to push my sexual buttons, but you don't have the first damn clue about what makes me happy. Today was a mistake—a mistake that will never happen again. You promised me. Give me your phone and let's say goodbye."

The bastard had the audacity to laugh. "Right. I don't think so, baby. I'll be in touch next time I'm in town. I'm sure you'll be bored enough with Vanilla by then to go another round or two with me."

Jake leaned down and gave Bri one last violent kiss before releasing her and walking to the door, leaving her alone without a backward glance. The heavy hotel door slammed closed, releasing a fresh wave of remorse. She let the sobs she'd tried to hold

LIVIA GRANT

back finally overcome her as she rolled into a ball on the king-sized bed.

There were so many thoughts swarming through her that it was hard for her to know what had her most upset. Was it the emotional and physical trials that Jake had put her through? Yes, he'd forced her, but even she knew it was her own mistakes that led her to this room. No one knew what Jake was capable of more than her. She'd been stupid enough to put herself into his path. Crushing guilt closed in.

But... the niggling fear fighting its way front and center was her worry that Jake just might be right—while she loved Markus with every fiber of her being, at the end of the day, his inability to please her sexually had the power to destroy their marriage in the long run.

After several minutes of wallowing in self-loathing, Bri forced herself to her feet, stumbling toward the bathroom for a quick shower but she gasped when she caught the first glimpse of her welted ass in the mammoth mirror.

"Damn you to hell for leaving marks, Jake," she spoke out loud to the empty room.

Markus' ringtone came from her bag just outside the bathroom door. He was calling her again, something he didn't often do in the middle of the day, particularly on court days. But it was getting late... and he was looking for her.

Sheer terror of losing him almost debilitated her. She waited until she heard the ding of the voicemail

62

he'd left for her before she rushed to the shower, turning on the water as hot as she could stand it before stepping into the spray. She needed to hurry, clean up, and get the hell out of there. She didn't want to call Markus back from the room in which she'd betrayed him.

CHAPTER SIX

TIFFANY

Tiffany pulled her cell phone out of her smock, checking to make sure she hadn't missed a call from Bri for the hundredth time that afternoon. It was getting late, and to say she was worried about her friend was the understatement of the decade.

She should've never let Bri leave with Jake Davenport. Regret for not calling the police when she had the chance closed in on her as she finished blow drying out one of Brianna's clients, which Tiff had been forced to take care of when her BFF had left her high and dry hours before.

After the customer paid and left, Tiff snuck back to the salon office so she could try to figure out what the hell to do. The final customers of the day were being taken care of by the remaining employees and it was getting late enough that the salon would be closing soon. There was absolutely no way that Bri could have been gone this long and not gone somewhere she shouldn't have with her ex. The thought of Bri going anywhere with the abusive asshole infuriated Tiffany.

How could she do this to me? To Markus?

She was just considering calling Markus back for help when the cell phone in her hand rang, making her jump.

She didn't even give Brianna a hello. "It's about damn time you phoned in," she answered angrily. "While you were out fucking around, your husband called here twice looking for you. Damn you for putting me in this position, Bri. I love Markus, and I hate having to lie to him."

Only when there was a long pause on the call did Tiff worry that it wasn't Bri at the other end of the phone. Did Jake have her phone?

"Brianna?" she said softer.

"I'm here. Please... what did you tell Markus?"

Tiffany's anger started to dissipate, replaced with concern for her best friend. She didn't sound good. She let out a long sigh before answering. "The first time I told him you were with a client and couldn't be disturbed, but when he called back again saying he couldn't reach you on your cell, I knew he wouldn't keep buying that. Do you have any idea how much I hated lying to him and telling him that you'd left early to go to the gym?"

Tiff heard the sigh of relief at the other end of the line. "Thank you so much for covering for me, Tiff.

That was a good idea about the gym. Did he believe you?" Bri's voice quavered.

"Of course, he believed me," she snapped. "He's a great guy who has no reason to think I would ever lie to him. And for the record, I really resent being dragged into this shit yet again."

Tiff could hear Bri start crying over her SUV's speaker. "I'm so sorry, Tiffany. Truly, I am. You're right, I'm a total idiot. I never should have left the shop today."

Brianna hadn't said it, but between the length of time she'd been gone and her current demeanor, Tiff had a pretty good idea what had happened. Still, she had to ask. "Did you get the evidence from him?"

Brianna's ugly chuckle gave her the unwelcome news, without using words.

Tiff pressed on, asking the next burning question. "Did he hurt you?"

"He..." Brianna sighed again, her voice cracking as she filled Tiff in. "Not any more than he used to."

"I don't want to hear about it. You're more than welcome to share the gory details of your sex life with Markus, but I prefer not to think of you and Jake together. It just pisses me off."

"I'm so sorry Tiff. Markus left me a voicemail. I'm supposed to meet him for dinner downtown in just over an hour. I know I'm supposed to close..."

Tiff was annoyed. "Bri, I told you that Jason and I were planning on going out tonight. I was supposed to be out of here already."

"I know... I wouldn't ask, but Markus..."

"I hardly think being late is gonna hurt him even close to as much as it will if he ever finds out where you've been and who you were with. Markus is perfect. He doesn't deserve this, Bri," Tiffany stated the obvious.

"I know... this was stupid. I thought I could get the hard drive and just make my past mistakes go away."

Tiff scoffed. "I told you not to go. He'll never give you the hard drive. But you never think straight when it comes to Jake." She hesitated, looking at the clock before giving in. "Go out tonight. Have dinner with your husband. Have a few drinks, get tipsy, and then you have to be honest with him about what it is you need that he isn't giving you. You have to give Markus a fighting chance to fill the need that's driving you to a creep like Jake."

A long pause followed by a loud sniffle came through the phone before Bri answered. "I know I need to. Markus is the antithesis of Jake. I just don't know how to tell him."

Tiffany sighed. "I get it. I really do. Gentle certainly has its place, but we both know you need more than that."

"I'd change it if I could..." Tiff could hear Bri's tears again through the speaker. "I don't want Jake. I *don't*. I want Markus. I just wish that Markus could fill that need for me. Does that make me selfish that I want it all?" A sob filled the car at Bri's end of the call.

"No, not selfish, but here's the thing, Bri, and there's no getting around it. You. Are. Married. And to an awesome guy who loves you very much. He's almost everything you ever wanted in a man. You need to open up and tell him about this and see if you can mold him into what you're missing. If you don't, you'll wake up one day and find out you've lost him."

"Don't you think I know that? Why do you think I went with Jake today? It was to get the stupid hard drive so we can put an end to this once and for all," Bri retorted defensively.

Tiffany cried bullshit. "Stop. We both know there's zero chance Jake will ever follow through on any promises he makes. He just strings you along because he knows once he gets you behind closed doors, he can take what he wants from you, and you won't do shit to stop him."

"Screw you, Tiff." Brianna spat.

"If you'd refused to go with him, it would be a moot point." When Bri was silent, Tiff took a deep breath before adding, "And I'm done covering for you with Markus. Today was the last time I'll lie to him for you. He deserves the truth... to be able to make things right."

When the call went silent, Tiffany hoped Bri was thinking about her advice and was relieved when her friend admitted, "Fine, I'll talk to him tonight."

"Yeah, right. How many times have I heard that

before, Bri?" She was tired of having the same conversation over and over.

"This is different."

"Sure, it'll be different until the next time Jake shows up."

"No, I'm done with him. You have no idea—"

"That's what you said six months ago, and then you went with him today. But sure, go out to dinner with your husband now and see if he can fill whatever hole Jake has been for you. Maybe then when the asshole comes back to town, you can tell him to fuck off." Tiff knew she was riding her best friend hard, but it had to be done.

Through the sniffles over the phone, Bri added quietly, "I'm hanging up now."

Tiff sighed. "Just talk to Markus before you ruin your marriage. Please."

"Bye Tiff. I'll see you tomorrow." The phone went dead.

Tiffany slid her phone into her pocket, trying not to feel guilty for how hard she'd been on her best friend. She was relieved that Bri was at least physically safe. Tiff was less sure about her friend's emotional state, particularly knowing how the guilt of what she'd done would weigh on Brianna.

She said a silent prayer that Bri would be brave enough to talk to her husband about what she needed from him and wasn't getting.

Even as she thought it, she admonished herself for being a hypocrite. She'd been dating Jason long enough to know without a doubt that he wasn't the right guy for her, but like Brianna, she'd been putting off being honest with him.

Maybe tonight she'd pluck up the courage to break up with him and move on herself.

Damn Brianna for not seeing how perfect her husband was. Tiff would give anything to find a man as perfect as Markus.

CHAPTER SEVEN

BRIANNA

The Uber app on Brianna's phone showed she was still eleven minutes away from the restaurant she was supposed to meet Markus at fifteen minutes ago. Her husband hated when she was running late, especially when he was stuck sitting at their table at Hugo's alone.

Brianna's heart thumped hard with crushing guilt. She'd had just enough time as she rushed to get ready to meet her husband for their celebratory dinner to know that as much as she'd love to blame Jake for what had happened in his hotel room that afternoon, she couldn't. Not completely. Sure, he'd been an asshole, and he'd tricked her... tied her down... forced himself on her.

And if he'd been a stranger, things would be different.

But he wasn't a stranger. She knew every evil trick in his dirty playbook and that meant she never should have left the shop with him. Looking back, it was so obvious.

Brianna shot off a text letting Markus know she was now nine minutes away, grateful that she'd been able to avoid speaking with him directly. They'd ended up leaving each other voicemail messages and texts to make the evening arrangements.

Today had made it clearer than ever that it was time to be honest with Markus. Even though Brianna found it almost impossible to ask her husband for the dark things her body craved—even if she felt shame for wanting them—she had to give him a chance. Tiffany's harsh words had hurt, but her best friend was right. Jake was a monster. Still, she had to acknowledge it was the act of being forced...utterly controlled and dominated... It was a better high than any high-priced pharmaceutical.

And she hated it.

She'd been successful for a few years at pushing her needs down deep, but there was no denying that Jake had a direct line to the part of herself she'd tried to bury with the end of their relationship.

And she *really* hated that.

Today was just another shining example of what a bastard he was.

By the time the driver pulled up in front of Hugo's, she was thirty minutes late.

"Thanks for the ride," she said as the doorman at the valet stand opened her car door for her. Bri made sure she had her phone and purse as she scrambled out of the back seat, wobbly on her high heels.

Her husband had requested she wear his favorite little black dress along with her red fuck-me pumps. He'd even asked her to wear the diamond necklace, earrings, and bracelet he'd gotten her for each of their three wedding anniversaries for their night out on the town. She'd done all she could to look her best in a desperate attempt to make the coming conversation easier.

As if me looking good makes a fucking difference.

Once inside the crowded lobby of the restaurant, Bri panicked. She'd been so focused on getting there, she'd neglected thinking about what she could possibly say to the man she loved more than anything else in the world when she saw him in a few minutes. As a woman brushed against her in the crush of waiting patrons, she could still feel the welts left on her ass by another man just hours before.

Tears blurred her vision.

I don't deserve him. I should tell him the truth, the minute I sit down. Tell him everything and beg for forgiveness.

She rejected the idea immediately. It was too risky. He'd never forgive her for what she'd done six months ago. How could he? She couldn't even forgive herself. But tonight, she would talk to him about what she was missing. Try to explain it to him. Maybe... just maybe... he might not think she was broken.

When it was her turn at the podium, she spoke

loud over the din of the crowd. "Hello. I'm Brianna Lambert. I'm meeting my husband for dinner. I'm incredibly late."

The regal maître d' gave the closest impression of a smile she'd ever seen from him on her many visits to her husband's favorite restaurant. "Of course, Mr. Lambert is waiting for you in his favorite booth. Peter here will take you to him. Enjoy your meal."

Brianna followed the server as he weaved them through the dining room tables full of tourists and families and into the smaller annex room near the back of the restaurant. The noise level dropped as the ambiance changed to intimate nooks and out of the way tables for two. She didn't need the escort. She knew the booth she'd find her husband in. It was the only place they'd ever sat on their many visits to his favorite restaurant.

Her first glimpse of Markus took her breath away. He was on his phone, looking off into the distance. Instinctively she reached out to grab the server's arm, stopping him from announcing her. He seemed to understand, leaving her to stand to the side, out of her husband's line of sight.

He was listening intently to whoever was on the other end of the line. He hadn't shaved like he normally did before going out in the evening. His dark facial hair grew back so fast, he often shaved twice in one day. Bri wanted to think he'd left his sexy scruff just for her since she told him often how much she loved this more dangerous looking Markus.

But it was the hard line of his jaw... the dark scowl as he listened that told her he didn't like what the person on the other end of the phone was saying.

Finally feeling stupid just standing there, she moved closer, catching his attention. As he turned toward her, she saw a darkness in his eyes she'd never seen before, but it was gone in a flash as recognition chased away the shadows from his gaze.

"Hey, need to go. Brianna's here."

Despite him saying he needed to hang up, the person on the other end of the phone kept talking for at least twenty seconds, leaving her standing awkwardly. When she finally started to sit at the end of the circular booth, Markus held up his hand, stopping her.

He never said goodbye to whoever he'd been talking with. He just pressed end and threw his phone to the table before sliding to the edge and standing.

Brianna fought the urge to cry tears of relief the second his arms hugged her tight against his chest. She buried her face against his dress shirt, taking in the hint of his cologne that she loved so much. She took a drag of his uniquely Markus scent, letting it calm her in a way she probably didn't deserve.

This... right here, in his arms, was where she belonged. She had to do whatever it took to make sure she never did anything that jeopardized her happily-ever-after with her husband ever again.

"God, I've missed you today," she offered truthfully

as she felt her husband's hands roaming lower from her waist to give her ass an indecent squeeze. Her squeal as he held her welted bottom was damning. She scrambled to cover her gaff. "I can't believe you're feeling me up in the middle of the restaurant."

Markus released her as she wiggled in his arms. When she pulled out of their embrace, he stayed close, glancing up and down, blatantly checking her out. His low whistle told her he approved of what he saw.

"Christ, you're a sight for sore eyes. After the day I've had, I've needed to hold you for hours." He turned and led her back to their booth, having her slide in first before he retook his seat on the end.

"I thought you had a good day," she prompted, reaching to take a sip of the already full water glass, hoping to calm her ragged nerves.

Just act normal.

"I did, for the most part. I never expected my court case to wrap up in one day. Honestly, it was a complete waste of time. The jury was out less than two hours before coming back in favor of my clients."

"That's great, honey. We need to celebrate tonight." Bri forced a smile.

"That's the plan. Dinner and a club." He paused before adding, "When you were late, I went ahead and ordered for you. David should be here any minute with your Cosmo and the appetizer."

She didn't say it, but she needed a strong drink.

She felt like she was going to jump out of her skin any minute. Guilt and fear of losing her marriage had her mind racing to find anything to talk about that would avoid her husband asking why he couldn't reach her earlier today.

I suck at lying.

"This sure beats last Friday night's Denny's dinner," she teased, trying to keep things light between them.

"If you didn't like Denny's, you shouldn't have picked it," he pointed out, grabbing a slice of the heavenly Italian bread they served at Hugo's.

"Yeah, well..." Brianna could hear Tiffany's voice in her ear, egging her on. "Maybe I just wanted you to pick the restaurant for us."

Markus finished his bite before defensively adding, "I just wanted you to pick a place that would make you happy."

Of course, he did. He always wanted her to be happy. Just like she got to pick the TV shows they watched. She decided on their menu at home. And what clothes she wore. And what to buy for the house. Where they vacationed. Brianna chided herself silently. She was the luckiest woman on the planet. Most women loved having control over everything in their life. She should just be happy and stop needing more.

"What?" Markus prompted when she didn't answer.

"Nothing," she said, reaching for her own bread just as David arrived with her drink.

Markus waited for their server to leave them alone before he pressed her. "You're quiet tonight. What's going on in that head of yours?"

Oh, he most definitely didn't want to know the answer to that question. "It's nothing."

"It sounds like something to me. You're never this quiet. On a normal night you'd be on your second or third story of what happened at The Beauty Box today. Everything okay with Tiffany?"

"Sure. We were just really busy today is all," she swallowed her bread and reached to take a long swig of her Cosmo.

"That's why I was surprised you had the time to go to the gym. You haven't been in weeks."

Stay calm.

"I know, but I need to get back into better habits," she offered truthfully.

"Well, I happen to like the way you look in my favorite little black dress."

Scrambling to change the subject from working out, she said, "I'm really glad we're going clubbing tonight after dinner. We haven't been dancing in forever."

Markus took a sip of his own cocktail before answering. "Yeah, well I figured it was about time I rectify that situation."

Their server arrived with the plate of fried calamari and the couple ate in silence for a few minutes. Brianna knew why she was struggling to come up with safe topics to talk about, but the silence wasn't like her normally jovial husband, either.

"You don't have to work this weekend, do you?" When he shook his head, she went on. "I was thinking after I get home from the salon tomorrow afternoon, maybe we could go to the nursery and pick out the flowers for the back yard. The landscapers are coming next week to plant the beds in the back."

"Let's wait and see how our day goes, okay?" he answered, taking another bite.

She tried not to be annoyed. "Sure... I guess." *Think. Another safe topic.* "I told you Sydney's wedding is coming up soon, right? I put it on the calendar on the fridge. I'm not sure when, but Kennedy is planning a bachelorette party for one of the upcoming weekends."

She looked up when she felt her husband's gaze on her. "A bachelorette party? I don't know... you think I can trust you to go out with the girls and not get into trouble?"

His words hit her hard. If he knew everything Jake was holding over her head, he would never trust her again. When she realized he was waiting for a response to his barb, she offered, "Tiffany will be with me. I'm sure she'll keep me out of trouble."

Markus's bark of laughter was out of place in the subdued upscale restaurant. "Somehow I doubt that. I'm pretty sure you two ladies have been getting in and out of trouble together since the day you met freshman year."

Brianna couldn't deny it since she'd shared all of their fun college stories with her husband. "Hey, we've matured. We're grown women now, not kids."

"All that means is you can get into grown-up trouble now."

It wasn't just her imagination. Their entire conversation since her arrival felt weird... awkward. It was just another thing to blame Jake Davenport for. Even hours after she was free of him, he'd taken up residence in her brain and was holding on for dear life.

Get the fuck out of my head, Jake.

By the time their entrees arrived, Bri and Markus's conversation skills had somewhat returned to normal, giving her a brief respite from her dark memories. Yet each time she looked for an opportunity to turn their discussion toward their sex life, or more specifically her darker sexual desires, she couldn't say the words.

By the end of the meal and two strong cocktails, Bri needed the ladies' room. Pushing to her feet, she felt wobbly on her heels. The alcohol was definitely helping ease her guilt. It made her ask, "Can you have David bring me one more Cosmo while I'm gone?"

Markus looked her over before asking, "You sure about that? I don't want you to faceplant on me before the night's over. I have plans for this body."

She loved the feel of his hands roaming up and down her back as he loosely hugged her to him. "I'm sure I can handle one more. But be warned, I plan on keeping my body close to yours all night when we're dancing at the club."

"Oh, I'm counting on it, sweetheart."

She saw a carnal darkness in his eyes. While it excited her, it was out of place for her husband in a public place.

Maybe he's had too much to drink himself.

Bri took off for the ladies' room, grateful for a few moments alone to regroup. She was exhausted from holding her guilt at bay—from keeping their conversation bouncing along in the safe zone, away from any topics that would bring her shame to light. It had taken her weeks to get back to normal the previous fall when Jake had first visited her. Without a doubt, she knew it would take even longer this time because she felt so foolish and angry at herself for being duped again.

By the time she felt steady again, she'd been gone for ten minutes and knew she couldn't stall any longer after she finished reapplying her lipstick and powdering her nose.

Speaking to her own reflection in the mirror, Brianna gave herself a pep talk. "Go out there and drink that Cosmo. Get tipsy and seduce your husband. Confess at least one thing it is you need from him."

But when she returned to their table, Markus was settling up their bill with their server.

"What, no Cosmo? No flourless chocolate cake for dessert?"

Markus glanced up after signing his name to the bill. "And here I thought you were trying to get back on track."

Instead of letting her slide back into the booth, he reached over to grab the shawl she'd worn to fend off the spring cool air.

"What's the rush?" she asked as he helped wrap her shawl around her shoulders, preparing to leave.

"We need to get to the club before nine," he answered, holding her elbow and moving them toward the exit.

"Since when do we need to hit a club that early?" She looked at her watch. "And how far away is it?"

"Not far," he answered as he handed his parking ticket stub to the uniformed valet just outside the restaurant door. Once the kid ran off in the direction of a nearby parking garage, Markus pulled her into his arms, hugging her to help keep the chill at bay. "I just want to get there early enough to get a good seat."

Seat? At a club? When Bri went dancing with Tiffany, they never sat down, but it had been forever since she'd been out on the town with her hubby. They were normally attending a stuffy law firm event or a wedding party.

She heard her husband's very expensive car before she saw the sporty Porsche come shooting out of the garage into traffic. Apparently, the valet dude was appreciating her husband's ride. When he pulled to a quick stop in front of them, Markus helped hold open the passenger door for Bri as she navigated her way into the low seat without flashing those passing on the sidewalk.

Markus gunned the engine as he pulled out into the Friday night traffic. They were close to the river, only blocks from Markus's office, so when he turned to head south and then west, Brianna was confused.

"Is the club in the suburbs?" she asked. Every dance club she'd ever been to in town was north, up in the nightlife district.

"Naw, but it's a bit farther out of the loop, in an up and coming neighborhood the city is revitalizing."

"That sounds like fun," Bri answered, trying to figure out how to jumpstart the difficult conversation they needed to have now that they had more privacy.

Go for broke. Just say it, Bri.

Taking a chance, she added softly, "Maybe if I dance too dirty, you can take me home and spank me."

She'd hoped he'd tease her about her uncharacteristic request. She'd have been happy with an inquiry back, asking why she'd said something like that. What she hadn't expected was silence as her husband stared straight ahead, navigating the traffic.

"Markus?" she prompted, reaching out to brush his arm. She could feel his muscles tensing under his dress shirt. He'd taken his suit jacket off and thrown it in the minuscule back seat.

"Why would you say something like that, Brianna? After all the abuse you went through before I met you, why the fuck would you joke about something like that?"

Stay calm. This is good. He's talking.

"Maybe I'm not joking. You're not like Jake..."

"Don't say the fucker's name. Not after how he hurt you."

"Okay... I won't. It's just..." Her words failed her. As always when she had to try to verbalize the insane things her body and mind craved, she came up empty. Admitting she wanted to feel pain—controlled pain—it was just wrong.

Markus filled the silence. "I made you a promise, didn't I? That I would never put you through the shit that asshole did." He glanced at her for the first time, and she saw his jaw locked, his eyes intense. "Haven't I kept up my end of the bargain?"

"You have... and I've loved you for it. Truly. I needed to heal, but..."

"There is no but, Brianna. You made it clear to me when we met that you'd been scarred, both physically and mentally, by what your ex put you through. I've seen the scars he left behind on your gorgeous body. I've held you as you woke up screaming from a nightmare. Forgive me if I'm a little confused by why you'd joke around about something so damn important."

Brianna was botching everything. She opened and closed her mouth, trying to come up with the right words, but they wouldn't come. Instead, tears blurred her vision and she had to swallow several times to keep from crying.

The rest of the short ride was in silence, each of them trying to figure out what to say to bring back the celebratory mood. By the time they turned into what felt like an industrial neighborhood, Bri was completely confused. Brick buildings that looked like old warehouses lined the streets, some with business signage on their entrances. While the landscaping and sidewalks had been refreshed and felt new, the neighborhood certainly wasn't a nightlife hub of the city.

She was just about to ask her husband if he was lost when he turned down a narrow alley between two warehouse-like buildings. There was barely enough room for two cars to pass in the block long path. From the street, she hadn't noticed that all of the street-level windows had been blacked out, making it impossible to see inside.

A single, well-lit awning jutted out from the brick building about halfway down. As they got closer, two burley men shot out of the heavy-looking, steel door. There was no signage, just a few letters and numbers that meant nothing to her.

TPP 7969.

If it weren't for the bulky bouncers and the

pounding music filtering out into the alley, Brianna never would have suspected they were at a club.

The men standing outside her car window made her nervous. They were looking through the tinted car window as if they were going to devour her. Brianna tore her eyes away from them to look at her husband.

"Markus, this is a strange location for a club. Are you sure you have the right address?"

He watched her closely as he replied, "Oh yeah, I'm sure."

"Well I'm not sure about this. What kinda club is it?"

"It's a private club. They have an exclusive kind of clientele."

Bri's heart rate had taken off. Something felt out of place... wrong. When her husband didn't expound on his comment, she prompted him. "And what kind of clientele is that?"

A strange expression broke out on his handsome face. "The naughty kind."

He didn't wait for a response. Instead, he exited the car, leaving her and her racing heart alone. She fought the urge to lock the car doors as her husband chatted with one of the guards. She strained to catch some part of their conversation but couldn't make out what they were talking about over the pounding bass coming from inside the club. She wasn't sure if she was relieved or not when Markus finally came around to open her door for her as one of the bouncers lowered himself into the driver's seat of the Porsche. He immediately had to move the seat back as far as it would go to try to make more room for his bulky body as he prepared to valet the car.

Brianna sat glued to her seat, afraid to get out. Something wasn't right. When Markus reached for her hand, she looked at him pleadingly, but refused to take his hand.

That was when she felt the bouncer's hand on her arm. He was gripping her hard enough that she worried he'd leave a bruise.

"I believe your husband is trying to help you out of the car, Mrs. Lambert. Why don't you be a good girl and listen." When she stayed frozen, he added a sharp, "Now."

Bri flinched and then scrambled to exit the car as fast as she could, wondering what she was getting herself into.

CHAPTER EIGHT

BRIANNA

Brianna huddled close to Markus as he closed the car door and the Porsche sped off down the alley. Only when the car turned out of sight did she realize that she'd left her purse with her phone in the car. She started to tell Markus that she needed her purse but decided against it as he hustled her toward the door, where the second menacing bouncer stood guard. He was as tall as Markus and covered in tattoos. Everything about him screamed danger.

When they got to the door, Markus reached to shake his hand. "Hey, Derek. Thanks for watching out for us."

"No problem, Markus. Anything for you, man." While he continued to pump Markus's hand in greeting, he let his eyes shift to Brianna and she was shocked at how brazenly he scanned her body. When she visibly shuddered under his gaze, the guard shot her a knowing smile and her shudder turned to a shiver.

Brianna grasped onto her husband's arm, trying to turn him toward her. She leaned closer to his ear. "Markus, I don't want to stay here. I know your friend invited us, but I'm not feeling well. Please... I want to go home now."

"Don't be silly, Brianna. We just got here. I can see you're cold. Let's get inside and we'll get you warmed up. I really think you're gonna enjoy it here." He shepherded her through the unmarked door, and she could feel Derek's eyes on her backside as they walked through a dimly lit hallway that opened to a round foyer that looked like it could have been in a different building altogether. The floor was mosaic marble, the walls hung with heavy, red velvet curtains similar to those used in old theaters. In the center of the room was a circular staircase leading to a second floor. A security keypad was on the wall next to the double doors Brianna assumed led into the main club judging by the techno music pounding beyond them.

Markus navigated the place like he'd been there before, holding Brianna's hand firmly as they headed up the stairs. She struggled to keep pace on the too-high stilettos he'd asked her to wear. She could sense Derek behind them, although she was afraid to look.

When they reached the top of the stairs, Derek moved around them, blatantly brushing against Brianna's body as he passed by. He took the lead as they walked down a shadowy, curved hallway. They passed numbered doors and Derek stopped when they reached the one labeled '3.' He produced a magnetic card and swiped it through the security pad next to the door. Once unlocked, he swung the door open and motioned for her to enter ahead of him.

Brianna tentatively went through the door, surveying the details of the unique room. There were four oversized, comfortable-looking chairs lined up in a semi-circle along the far wall, curiously facing away from the door. As she went a few feet into the room she understood why. The far end of the room was open to the large first floor and as she approached the back of the stuffed chairs, she saw they were standing in a private balcony box overlooking the club below. She could see the large, fully stocked bar as well-dressed men milled about waiting for drinks. Her attention was drawn to the two-story, red velvet theater curtains that were drawn across a mammoth, slightly curved stage that ran the entire length of the room opposite the observation boxes.

Brianna moved between the chairs to stand near the railing. A Plexiglas panel beneath the railing allowed for better viewing of the club seats below for those in private box chairs. From this vantage point, she could see much more of the first floor. She'd expected theater-style seating since they were in an auditorium. Instead she saw multiple areas with comfortable chairs and couches along with tables of varying shapes and sizes, artfully arranged for a casual feel. Only when leaning far over the railing could she make out several rows of true theater-style rows located directly under the second-floor private boxes.

While she didn't see a dance floor or dancers, the pounding dance music continued to play. Brianna became increasingly uneasy when she evaluated the occupants of the room below. There were over a dozen powerful-looking men milling about, as if at a cocktail party. Beside them were women in varying degrees of undress, all kneeling next to the men.

Her mind reeled; had her gentle husband brought her to a sex club?

Excitement overshadowed her nagging fear as Brianna saw another couple arrive and walk up to the group below. After shaking hands with a few of the men, the well-dressed older man turned to the woman next to him and helped her to take off the long coat she was wearing. Brianna's breath caught when she saw the woman was completely naked under the coat except for a leather collar and wrist and ankle cuffs. Her eyes were riveted as the man took what appeared to be a leash out of his suit pocket and attached it to the thick leather collar snuggly fastened around the woman's neck. As soon as the leash was attached, Brianna watched the blonde woman fall gracefully to the floor into a kneeling position. Her legs were spread apart as she leaned back and clasped her hands behind her neck, proudly displaying her naked body to anyone who

LIVIA GRANT

glanced her way. The man holding her leash—
presumably her Master—continued to talk with the
other men. He occasionally reached his hand down to
gently stroke the hair of the beautiful slave
obediently kneeling next to him.

Brianna's pussy was throbbing with an onslaught
of desire as she watched the scene play out in front of
her. Cocktail waitresses in body-hugging corsets
made their way through the crowd, taking drink
orders and delivering appetizers and beverages to the
Masters and Mistresses in attendance. Bri couldn't
help but notice that the corsets stopped short of
covering the server girls' breasts, but rather served as
shelves to push their naked breasts up and out for all
to admire. Even from this distance Bri could make
out the heavy-duty nipple piercings that decorated
the servers' perky tits.

She was so lost in thought as she took in the scene
below that she didn't hear Markus come up behind
her. She gasped with surprise as he placed his hands
on her hips, yanking her against him. She moaned
when she felt his raging hard-on pressing tightly
against her ass. He slipped his arms around her,
holding her tightly.

"How do you like the club so far?" he asked.
"They put on a show every night. I think you're really
gonna find it interesting, sweetheart."

Bri tried to turn around so she could see him, but
Markus held her tightly facing forward, forcing her to
watch as things continued to unfold below. She

observed, mesmerized as most of the men took seats in the various furniture groupings close to the stage. Their leashed slave girls crawled along behind them and most knelt at the feet of their seated Master.

An older dark-haired dominant pulled the leash of his red-headed slave closer, pointing briefly to his crotch. Even from a distance, Brianna saw the satisfied smile adorning the face of the naked slave girl as she reached out and began to undo her Master's fly, releasing him from the confines of his pants. After giving his semi-hard cock a few strokes with her hand, she dove in and greedily took the entire length of him into her mouth. Her Master continued talking with the other men seated nearby as if nothing were happening. His only acknowledgement of the blowjob he was receiving was the placement of his hand on his submissive's head as she bobbed up and down.

Brianna's heart was racing. She was so turned on by the scene playing out below that she could feel herself flooding her lacy panties. Her breathing was becoming increasingly short and labored the longer she drank in the sights. Markus's hard tool pressing tightly against her back was the icing on the cake. She still hadn't said a word. Her mind was reeling at the possible implications.

"Markus, why did you bring me here? This is obviously a sex club. We've never gone to a club like this."

He continued to hold her against him painfully

tight as he whispered into her ear. "I had a feeling you might enjoy a little entertainment like this, sweetheart. Tell me Brianna, are you getting turned on by what you see?"

Her uncertainty with this new Markus made her want to say no, but her body was giving her away. She was especially confused considering their brief conversation in the car on the way here, yet, he couldn't possibly miss her lusty scent wafting up from her now drenched panties. Her body had begun to subtly rub against her husband's hard-on pressed into her bottom. Occasional low moans escaped from between her lips as she watched the slave girl below getting a full-force face fucking. Her Master was giving her blowjob his full attention now as he roughly pushed her face down so hard that Brianna could clearly see her gagging. The lighting was just right to catch the wet tears streaming down the slave's cheeks from her exertion and the hard use.

Markus reached up to grab Bri's right breast just as the Master below grabbed the hair of his red-headed submissive, holding her tightly against his cock, her nose touching his stomach as he spurted his cum deep down her throat. Brianna could see the look of panic on the girl's face as she was unable to catch a breath. Just when it seemed as if she may faint, her dominant finally pulled his cock from her mouth, allowing her to gasp wildly for air. She sputtered for a few seconds before recovering enough to show her Master the remaining cum pooling in her now open mouth before he waved his hand, presumably giving her permission to swallow.

The floor below was quickly filling up with new arrivals. The latest two couples to arrive were clearly two dominant Mistresses with boy-toys on leashes. The older of the two slave boys was wearing a cock ring. His tool was long and hard and it looked like it was ready for action at a moment's notice. He was wearing open-ass leather chaps that displayed his red butt, heavily scored with what looked like cane welts. The sight of the welts reminded Bri of her belting at the hands of Jake earlier. She emitted a guttural moan that she hoped Markus thought was due to his pinching her nipple through the fabric of her dress.

The second Mistress was dressed in a black leather corset that accentuated her huge breasts. She was heavily tattooed and wore fishnet stockings and carried a riding crop in her left hand, pulling her young slave boy behind her with her right. He looked absolutely pitiful. Bri suspected that he couldn't be older than twenty. Judging by the wicked welts on his naked back and ass, it was clear that he'd recently been disciplined, and his punishment was ongoing; the slave boy's cock and balls were tightly encased in a chastity belt, probably to keep him from touching himself. He also wore a harness around his waist. Straps running from its D-rings ran between his legs to his ass and appeared to be holding in a dildo or large butt plug. The young man's only other adornments were his wrist and ankle restraints and, of course, his collar. His Mistress took the time to unhook the leash from his collar and moved the clasp down to attach it to a hook on his cock ring. As she took off toward the bar, she yanked on the leash, pulling her slave boy behind her by his tortured cock.

Unable to contain herself any longer, Brianna reached her hands behind her to grasp her husband's hips as he humped her through their clothes. She threw her head back to lean it against his shoulder while he groped her breasts roughly. She may have been getting over-heated with the sexy scenes surrounding her, but she was smart enough to know that tonight was her chance. She had no clue why Markus thought she might enjoy coming to a club like this, but at the moment she didn't care what his reasons were. Now that they were here, she had her opening to confess to him that she needed him to dominate her, at least sometimes, like the slave girls below. She had a quick shot of hope that Markus would be able to fulfill all of her sexual desires so she could purge her desire for Jake's dominance once and for all.

Bri let out a loud moan as Markus lowered his lips to her sensitive neck and began torturing her with the lethal combination of alternating sucks bordering on bites and sweet, tender kisses. Before long, she was sure he was leaving his mark on her neck and she loved it.

Markus lowered his left hand to the hem of her dress, pushing it up to gain access to her sex hidden by her skimpy panties. He only had time to stroke the length of her sopping pussy once before the lights in the theater flickered. While the people standing below them moved toward the couches and chairs to get settled for the upcoming show, her husband continued to finger her wet folds while pinching her right nipple harder than he ever had before.

Bri's core lit on fire at his touch. Her cunt literally throbbed with her desire to be taken. Markus appeared to know what she needed as he finally brushed her clit, causing Bri to shiver with delight in his arms. At first his brushes were light and teasing, not nearly enough to push her over the cliff to a climax, but just enough to bring her to the edge. As she rubbed her ass up and down over his hard cock, she closed her eyes, blocking out everything but the feel of his fingers on her body.

Just as she was about to come, Markus unbelievably removed his hands from her pussy and nipple and simply hugged her around her waist, keeping her close to him. Bri let a groan of frustration escape just as she felt slippery fingers invading her lips. She could taste her own excitement on Markus's fingers and was amazed how turned on she got being forced to suck his fingers clean.

Brianna finally opened her eyes to look over to the box to their left, where she could hear—and vaguely see—people having sex. She just made out the shape of a naked woman bent over the railing in front of the box seats. A large, fully clothed man was pounding an attractive middle-aged blonde hard and fast from behind. The woman had a mixed look of pain and pleasure as her dominant grabbed her hips, riding her hard. The women's eyes met and they shared an unexpected moment of sisterly camaraderie. Brianna watched almost jealously as her neighbor got fucked exactly the way she loved the best—hard and fast.

Unable to look away, Brianna continued her role as voyeur until Markus's tight squeezing of her hip got her attention. For the first time since their arrival, he loosened his grip on her enough to spin her around to face him. When she raised her eyes to meet his gaze, she was overwhelmed by the mixed look of sadness and anger floating in his deep brown eyes. They continued to stare into each other's eyes for several long seconds before Markus questioned her. "Why didn't you tell me before that you get turned on by rough sex, Brianna? I thought after your ex hurt you, you hated the idea of being dominated, of being hurt."

She was flustered. She didn't expect these questions. She fidgeted before finally answering truthfully. "I love you, Markus. I love how you hold me gently when you make love to me. It's just..." She lost her nerve and looked away, glancing back to watch the woman getting plowed.

Markus reached up to touch her chin, pulling her to face him again. His hand stayed under her chin, tenderly stroking her cheek as they continued to search each other's eyes for answers. They were trying to make sense of the raging emotions running through them as they evaluated what they'd learned about the other since their arrival.

Through halting uncertainty, Bri finally got the courage to stumble through a somewhat disorganized rant. "Just sometimes... I guess— Well, I really would like it if you would... be more aggressive. At home. In the bedroom. I want you... no... I *need* you to dominate me. You know... spank me and stuff. At least sometimes."

After her confession, he remained silent.

As his eyes bored into her, she quietly asked her own burning question. "How did you know that I would even be open to coming to a place like this, Markus?"

His face turned to sheer pain before he replaced it with a hard, determined facade. When he spoke, he ignored her question completely and his tone was hard, angry. "You should have told me Brianna. You should have fucking told me a long time ago."

His anger rekindled her fear. Was it possible he knew about Jake? Why else would he bring her here and ask her these things? Her mind raced to find a way to explain her unforgivable behavior, but before she could reply, the entire room was thrown into pitch darkness. The techno dance music had stopped, replaced with the heavy beating of drums and a lone electric guitar.

Markus had released her chin and they both

turned their attention to the stage where the curtains pulled open. Brianna's stomach dropped when she saw that the stage was basically one huge dungeon. It looked like a scene straight out of medieval times, or a BDSM porn movie. The St. Andrew's cross along the back wall caught Bri's attention first, but as she allowed her eyes to glance quickly across the stage, she was shocked to see a whipping post in the middle of the stage, and an already occupied pillory.

The naked slave girl whose wrists and head were locked into the wooden stockade structure appeared to have been there for some time. She struggled to keep her balance, and each time she began to collapse, the heavy weights clamped to her nipples and labia swayed, causing her face to grimace in pain. Her legs were being forced uncomfortably wide apart by a wooden spreader bar attached to her ankle restraints. Even with the dim lighting, it was clear she'd been crying as her face was puffy and red.

Until Brianna noticed this small detail, she'd assumed they were here to watch a pre-planned and rehearsed sex show, but something in the way the submissive was behaving set off more alarm bells with Brianna. She had a sudden fear that what they were about to witness was less about rehearsed play, and more about real-life punishment, and that terrified her.

Finally dragging her attention away from the suffering slave girl, Brianna took in the spanking bench made from a sawhorse with a padded top.

Heavy leather straps hung from the padded arm and leg rests and looked sturdy enough to immobilize the strongest of spanking victims. Brianna's pussy almost convulsed at the thought of Markus strapping her into the cruel device and lighting up her ass with a heavy paddle or belt. She was so turned on that she stumbled backwards against her husband's chest. Sweet relief washed over her as he wrapped his arms around her protectively, holding her to him.

Bri forced herself to move from the tempting spanking bench to a nearby diabolical-looking gynecological exam table. The stirrups were high and wide, with heavy locking straps and rings to immobilize recalcitrant patients. A huge red enema bag hanging from a wheeled stand sat waiting by the bed, along with a cabinet filled with probing medical instruments.

Near the medical scene was what looked to be a tall stool with a padded backrest. The subject sitting in the chair would have their legs pulled wide apart and strapped down at the thighs in a similar fashion to the medical table stirrups. At first Brianna didn't understand this device's purpose, but then she noticed the five-gallon bucket placed directly under the opening of the stool seat, and realized this chair was meant to restrain anyone unlucky enough to release their enema on stage for all to see. The mere thought of witnessing—let alone being forced to participate in—such a humiliating punishment caused Brianna's knees to buckle underneath her. If not for Markus's supporting embrace, she would have crumpled to the floor.

Bri was transfixed as she took it all in. Her thoughts were a whirl of fear, doubt and—against her better judgment—excitement. There was no denying the scene below had unleashed a torrent of submissive feelings in her. She wanted to turn around and beg Markus to take her down to the stage and use every torturous device on her. After all, she'd felt overwhelming guilt all day since her time with Jake. In her heart, even though she could blame it on being blackmailed and tricked by her ex, she knew she deserved to be punished by her husband. But even as she considered this, she remembered what he had told her in the car: he wasn't that kind of man. He was tender to a fault.

So why did Markus bring her to this club?

It was clear he knew the bouncer and it almost seemed as if he'd been here before, which meant he *knew* this was a BDSM sex club. She just couldn't reconcile the gentle Markus she was married to with the man standing behind her right now. Regardless, she realized she was grinding her legs together in an attempt to get friction to her neglected clit. She was ready to combust from the growing sexual need and Markus ran his hand up her thigh until he grazed her sensitive nub. The second he brushed her clit, she groaned with pleasure.

In a tone she had never heard him use, Markus commanded, "Take off your panties. Right now."

Without hesitation, Brianna blurted out, "Yes, sir." The submissive response seemed so natural to her. She was more than happy to comply and hoped he planned on plunging his rock-hard cock into her. Once she handed the scrap of fabric to her husband, he slipped her panties into his pocket.

Before Brianna could beg Markus to take his cock out of his pants and impale her, her attention was drawn to a bulk-of-a man entering the stage through a door at the back near the St. Andrew's cross. The guy had to be at least six foot two, with dark, thick hair that just brushed his shoulders. He had a five o'clock shadow, tanned and tattooed skin, and carried himself as if he owned the world. He was dressed simply in well-worn jeans and a black tee shirt that showcased his broad shoulders, muscular arms, and trim waist. Bri didn't miss the riding crop hanging from a hook on his wide leather belt.

When he spoke, it was clear he had a wireless microphone attached to him because his voice boomed throughout the club. "Members, welcome back to The Punishment Pit!" The music softened as he began to talk and Bri wondered if he was an announcer about to welcome actresses and actors to the stage for a BDSM role-play performance. "You picked a great night to be with us because we have some very naughty boys and girls tonight in need of proper punishment. You're also all in for a special treat as we welcome an old friend of mine back into the club. He's come to me with a problem he needs my help in solving. I think you're all going to enjoy watching me do just that." An evil grin lit up his handsome face as he very clearly raised his eyes up to stare directly into their private box.

As his words started to sink in, Bri reluctantly turned around to look at Markus. His eyes were dark and hard, tinted with a hint of pain. He seemed about to say something but stopped and looked at the stage before turning back to his wife. Brianna was beginning to feel sick to her stomach by the time he finally addressed her.

"You've been a very naughty girl, Brianna."

Her heart dropped. He knew.

CHAPTER NINE

BRIANNA

Brianna's mind was racing. How could Markus have possibly found out about Jake? Her first instinct was to try to declare her innocence and deny any wrongdoing, but it only took a few torturously long seconds to know that route would only make things worse. There was no denying the pain and hurt in her husband's eyes, and she knew it was too late to feign innocence. Still, maybe he didn't know everything. Maybe he just knew that she hadn't been where she said she'd been this afternoon. Even if he somehow knew that Jake had come to the salon looking for her, he couldn't possibly know where they'd gone or what they'd done together? Could he know she'd been blackmailed by her ex?

The rest of the club melted away for Brianna. She turned her focus on Markus, searching his eyes for any hint of softness or love, any hint of what he might know. What she saw was a stranger staring back at her. Markus's face was a mask of anger. With each passing second, she could see his resolve strengthening and she watched with growing terror as the last remnants of his pain and hurt were replaced by a steely hardness.

By the end of the longest minute of her life, Bri was physically ready to collapse under the weight of her fear and guilt. She had to dig deep to find her shaky voice. "Markus... honey... please talk to me. What's happening?"

"Oh, I think you know exactly what's happening, Brianna. You did, after all, put this entire night into motion with your traitorous actions, didn't you?" Markus waited several long seconds before confirming her worst fear. "I sure hope he was a great fuck since he's gonna cost you everything." His voice dripped with venom.

Until now, Brianna had been in shock—too afraid to internalize what was happening to her. Now her body began to quake with fear as hot tears flooded her eyes, spilling down her cheeks. A rush of overwhelming guilt and self-loathing rocked her to her core.

She didn't remember making a conscious decision to throw herself at his mercy. In fact, she didn't remember much about those first fateful minutes of her doom. All she knew was that when she emerged from her trance, she was at her husband's feet with her arms wrapped around his legs, holding on for dear life.

"Markus, I'm so sorry! I swear to you, I love you so much! You have to believe me. I'm so very sorry! I didn't want to go. It's just that he has info... damning... shit... believe me, honey... I just wanted to protect us... I am so sor—"

"Enough! It's too fucking late. I don't believe anything you have to say. Let go of me." He easily tore her away from him, roughly shoving her backwards. She fell on the floor behind the balcony seats, her short dress riding up enough to give her husband a glimpse of her bare pussy.

Markus squatted in front of her, reaching out to roughly grab her cunt. He squeezed her sex with all of his strength. "Did you like having someone else's cock in here today, Brianna? Is he bigger than me? Harder? What the hell does he have that I don't?" The pain in his voice broke her heart into a million pieces.

She begged through her sobs. "Markus... truly... I'm so very sorry. Please believe me, you're the only man I love. Please, can't we go home and talk about this there? I swear to you, I'll tell you everything. I'll spend the rest of my life making this up to you. I need you. I lo—"

"Shut the fuck up, Brianna! I don't believe a single word coming out of your whoring mouth. The second you let another man shoot his cum into your body is the second you lost the right to tell me you love me." He shook his head, as if he couldn't believe he had ever trusted her. "I have to hand it to you, Bri.

107

I really did think you were different, but you're just another gold-digging bitch. Well, bad news for you. You're about to lose your free ride, baby."

His voice and words may have been vicious, but the tears streaming unchecked down his face showed how devastated Markus was by her unexpected betrayal.

Brianna continued begging through her sobs. "I don't care about your money! Take back the salon, the car, the jewelry, the clothes—take it all! I just want you Markus... please."

"You have a pretty sick way of showing it," Markus scoffed. His grip on her pussy was like a vice.

"You're hurting me, Markus. Please. Let's go home and talk about this." Brianna was trying to push away from him, trying to loosen his grip on her tender parts.

"Oh, you don't know what hurt is yet, Brianna." His words were ominous and jolted Brianna back to the here and now. She suddenly heard the sounds she'd blocked out—sounds of the punishment club. She'd been so focused on getting through to Markus she'd tuned out everything around her. Now she was acutely aware that somewhere below, a woman was screaming.

The relief of Markus finally releasing his grip on her was short lived when he roughly grabbed her by her upper arms, yanking her to her feet. In one swift move, he swung her around forcibly to face the stage. She briefly tried to struggle free, but he gripped her in a death lock, forcing her to witness the scene playing out on the main floor. In spite of her discomfort, she was relieved he was touching her, holding her tightly against his hard body, even if only in anger.

He leaned in close to whisper against her ear. "Are you watching, Brianna? Do you see what happens to cheating whores?"

Brianna knew she should be horrified, but as she watched she was torn between terror and delirium. It was like watching a scene from her favorite tattered erotic romance novel—a book that had fed her masturbatory fantasies since college.

On the stage below, a naked slave girl had been trussed up, her arms attached to rings at the top of a whipping post. Her position facing the stage allowed the audience to catch the back of her body as the hulky bouncer Derek punished her.

The slave girl's legs were splayed wide open by a spreader bar and Brianna watched in horrified fascination as her punisher used a bullwhip to stripe her back, ass, and legs. Even from the relatively long distance, Bri saw the ugly welts blooming across the poor woman's body. It was clear Derek was a master at his craft; he was causing great pain without creating open wounds, which could easily happen with such a deadly implement.

After a final stroke of the whip that wrapped around the poor slave's ass and drew an agonizing scream from his victim, Derek threw the whip down and stepped up close to examine his handiwork. He was surprisingly tender as he gently caressed the submissive girl's ass, leaning in to place a kiss on her cheek. The sobs were still racking her small body when the Master on stage spoke again.

"I'm sure slave Cindy is already regretting her continued acts of defiance against her Master, but as this is her second offense, Master Michael has asked Derek to make sure her lesson *takes* this time."

The gasp from the submissive on stage was audible as he took a short break before continuing.

"I sentence slave Cindy to another twelve strikes with the wooden paddle and we'll end with twelve strokes of the cane. The sentence will be carried out in phases throughout the evening. Let her think about her sins for a while on the whipping post before we move her to the spanking bench for the rest of her sentence."

Only now did Brianna see that the Master in charge was actually seated in what looked exactly like an eighteenth-century-era throne on a raised platform toward the left of the stage.

"Master Peter, I believe you have a matter you'd like to bring to our attention tonight. Please join me on the stage."

There was a commotion in the pit below. Brianna saw a man that must have been Master Peter pulling on the leash of a redheaded submissive who'd been sitting quietly at his feet. Now that they'd been called to the stage, the submissive had come alive. Her cursing could be heard throughout the club. After failing to get the naked submissive to follow him up on stage, Peter proceeded to unbuckle his wide leather belt and apply it to her ass with quick, hard strokes. The submissive let out a yelp and finally made her way to the stage, begging for mercy all the way.

"I'm so sorry Master," she cried. "I truly am sorry. Please, can't we go home? I'll be a good girl."

By the time they were in front of the head Master, Brianna could see Master Peter was visibly softened by his slave's pleas. As he gently reached down to wipe tears from her cheeks, Brianna wondered if he might relent, but then the head Master reminded everyone why the couple is on stage.

"Master Peter, please share with everyone why you've asked that slave Kristen be punished tonight."

Peter turned to face the crowd. "As you know, I collared her over three months ago in a ceremony on this very stage. At the time we entered into a total power exchange 24/7 relationship. Since then, it's become clear that Kristen doesn't have a submissive bone in her body. I'm beginning to fear she's interested in just one thing—my money. It just came to my attention that in the space of three months, she's spent over thirty-thousand dollars on clothes, jewelry, and who knows what else. I'm here to ask you to punish her severely in the hopes that she can be reformed."

LIVIA GRANT

The Master's tone was sympathetic. "Master Peter, she certainly deserves to be punished, but seriously—if she's broken so many rules in your Master/slave contract, why not just cut your losses and release her?"

Master Peter glanced down at the crying slave at his feet and then back at the Master on his throne. "God help me, but I love her. I'd like to at least try to train her properly. I know she needs a stronger hand to get her on track and that's why I'm bringing her to you and Master Derek. I'll defer to any training you suggest."

Kristen was holding onto her Dom's leg as if to throw herself at his mercy, much like Brianna had done with Markus just minutes before. "No Peter, please! I love you so much! Please don't—"

The Master on stage silenced her with a loud, "Enough!" The warning stopped her pleas but not the tears. "Slave Kristen, I want to remind you that you do have an option here. As your Dominant, Peter has brought you here to punish you and get your training back on track. I'm sure you remember the details of the contract you signed when you agreed to be Master Peter's submissive and a member of our club. You chose a safeword that can be invoked to stop your punishment immediately. However, failing to submit to your Master publicly will not only negate your contract but lead to banishment from the club."

He smiled at Kristen's distressed look. It was easy to see that she hated both her options.

The dominant men on stage gave the crying submissive an agonizingly long minute to contemplate her fate. When she finally raised her eyes from the floor, she looked at Peter. "I love you, Sir. Please forgive me. I promise to do better."

Brianna could see the pain crossing the Dom's face as his sub begged for his forgiveness, but the Master of Ceremonies didn't allow Peter to relent.

"No more whining. Master Derek, gag her and let's get her settled onto the bench for starters."

Master Derek was already in motion and effortlessly picked up the petite, redheaded girl and threw her over his shoulder, giving her bare ass several open-handed swats as he marched over to the spanking bench. He made quick work of pushing her body down over the padded top and tightly securing first her arms and then her legs to the heavy piece of furniture. A final leather strap was brought across her body at her waist to immobilize her further.

Kristen continued to cry out for Peter to rescue her, but Master Derek stopped her begging by inserting a ring-gag into her mouth, forcing her to open wide. Drool ran down her chin as Derek affixed a wide collar that caused her head to stay upright, giving the entire audience a clear view of her face throughout the punishment.

Brianna's heart was racing as she took in the scene

below. Markus had continued to hold her tightly against him, making her face the unfolding drama below. Little did he know how grateful she was for his touch. Her legs felt like they could crumble beneath her any minute. She took time to close her eyes and tried to calm herself. She needed to think of how she could possibly fix things with Markus. She was finding it hard to think of a way out because she knew how very hurt she would've been if he'd done the same thing to her.

How could I have been so stupid? I hurt the person who loves me most in this world, and for what? Impersonal, hot sex with an abusive ex-boyfriend. It doesn't matter what he's blackmailing me with. My God, I don't deserve Markus's forgiveness.

Her attention was brought back to the scene on the stage below by the agonized screams coming from the wayward submissive who was in the process of getting a butt-blistering paddling, administered by Master Derek. He was using what appeared to be a wooden fraternity paddle with multiple round holes drilled through it. Brianna was absolutely ashamed that the sound of the wood meeting flesh was causing her pussy to throb. The slave girl's gag-mumbled screams combined with her groans of pain sent an electric jolt straight to Brianna's core.

After at least twenty-five licks of the paddle, Derek stopped long enough to move closer to admire his work. He lightly caressed the naughty girl's ass, allowing her time to slow her sobbing and gain some level of control over herself. Bri could see marks on her wrists where she'd been jerking wildly against the restraining straps, desperate to be free.

The punishment already seemed severe to Brianna so when Master Derek moved to the nearby table to trade his punishment implement in for another, Bri almost collapsed. Markus held her upright and facing forward as she watched Derek return to the occupied spanking bench. He took the time to turn the bench a quarter turn in order to give everyone watching a new angle for viewing. He then proceeded with the punishment, this time using a riding crop. He set a slower pace, stopping to caress the naughty slave's back in a calming manner every third stroke or so. The care he seemed to be taking to ensure no permanent damage was comforting, and yet felt somewhat out of place to Brianna.

Red welts now crisscrossed Kristen's buttocks and the final three hard strokes were centered on the tender sit spot where her ass meets her thighs. Her blood-curdling screams through her open gag let all spectators know how painful they were. Her body was now physically shaking from the strain of fighting her restraints and the overwhelming pain consuming her naked body.

Derek had laid the crop down on the nearby table and returned to once again massage the slave girl's punished parts. When he dipped his hand across her wide-open pussy, he chuckled. "I think she's actually liking her punishment, Peter. She's dripping wet. We'll try to get her back on track tonight, but it's clear you're going to need to perform regular maintenance punishments to keep her behaving."

Derek returned to the table to pick up his next implement—a leather strap that was a couple feet long and about two inches wide. He took a minute to test the strap against his own leather-covered thigh and once satisfied it was what he was looking for, he returned to a calmer Kristen. He rotated the spanking bench a quarter turn again to give the spectators a new viewing angle.

He made sure to show Kristen the next tool he'd chosen and her cry of fear resounded through the room. Master Derek moved closer to her and placed a hand on her lower back, caressing her until her fear was under control.

Unfortunately for her, the respite was short lived. Derek brought the strap down across her ass over and over. While he'd given time between strokes before, he was now acting like a man on a mission, using his full strength to lob smacks across her beet-red ass. Ugly stripes covered her bottom and thighs from the little dimples above her ass all the way to just above her knees.

The screams coming from the naughty slave on the stage were horrific and Brianna was shaking so hard now that she finally collapsed against her husband. Bri was sobbing at the mere thought that Markus might allow the barbarians on the stage to do to her what they were doing to the current occupant of the bench.

Through her sobs Brianna resumed appealing to her spouse. She tried to turn around so she could face him, but he refused to loosen his grip, forcing her to continue to watch the scene below. "Markus, please. I'm begging you. Please let's go home. You can give me any punishment you feel necessary, but please... you can't let them do this to me." She would have kept begging, but her sobs took over and Brianna found she could no longer force the words out of her bone-dry mouth. Her full weight was now being supported by her strong husband, but when she moved to cover her ears to drown out the tortured sobbing from below, he pulled her arms tightly behind her back to further immobilize her. When she tried to look away, he grabbed her hair and forced her to watch the whipping continue below.

While he held her head still, she was able to at least divert her eyes from the stage to the other spectators on the main level. To her amazement, she saw more than one couple fucking as they watched the punishment continue. Two submissives were draped over their Doms' laps getting their own bare-ass spankings.

Bri's fear of what was going to happen to her and Markus was palpable. To cope, she shut down, blocking out the violence happening all around her. She was scared, and so confused. Her guilt was overwhelming, but she truly had no one to blame but herself if her husband walked out of her life without a backward glance. Still, she was terrified of losing Markus.

But layered on top of that fear was her deep, dark secret. Her body was already betraying her as she could feel her juices flowing freely between her legs. With each slap of the strap against the flesh on stage, Bri became more aware of her own wetness dripping down her inner thighs. The only thing flowing harder were her tears of regret.

Markus

Markus was in denial as the scent of his wife's arousal surrounded them. He released his grip on her hair, shoving his left hand under the hem of her dress and roughly plunging two fingers deep into his wife's dripping cunt.

"I can't fucking believe you, Brianna. I bring you here to scare the shit out of you as punishment for trashing our marriage, and instead you're getting turned on. I'm beginning to think I don't know you at all." Markus stilled the pumping of his fingers. The couple were both suspended there, connected in body as they watched Master Derek flaying the wayward submissive on the stage. Disgusted with his own sexual arousal, Markus shoved Bri away from him hard enough that she fell forward across the back of the couch in front of them.

It tore at his heart when she buried her head into the cushion, sobbing. Desperation, anger, and fear merged into a dangerous cocktail that had him unzipping his pants and whipping out his hard rod.

He gave her no warning before thrusting balls-deep inside her. The brutal insertion of his rock-hard cock was meant to be a punishment for his wife. It made him an even bigger asshole that he reveled in Brianna's resulting scream which had to have been heard by everyone in the club.

If members could peek into their private box, they would spy a determined man pounding his wife at a brutal pace. Rage rolled off his body as he viciously dug his grip into her hips, yanking her body back hard to meet his forward thrusts. There was no love in this coupling, only pain and betrayal. It was meant to be the ultimate punishment fuck, but within minutes Brianna's moans of ecstasy as she exploded in a powerful orgasm showed Markus firsthand how little he understood his wife's sexual needs. Her previously guilty sobs had been replaced with a litany of dirty talk that would make a truck driver blush—or at least want to jack-off.

"Oh, my God. That's it Markus... fuck me hard. Yes! Harder! That's it, honey... oh God... thank you. I needed this so bad. I'm so sorry... so very sorry. I love you so much. That's it... fuck me harder... yes..." Her rambling became incoherent as she rolled into her next orgasm, her pussy squeezing his shaft as her juices spilled down between them. She melted down into a sexual mess like he'd never seen.

Witnessing his wife come unglued before his very eyes pushed Markus into the most explosive orgasm of his life. His heart felt like it could pound right out of his chest between his physical exertion and his precarious emotional state. As he stayed buried balls-deep in his wife's traitorous pussy, the dam holding his emotions at bay finally collapsed and the fearless defense attorney who could eat opposing council for lunch found himself crying hot tears as he grappled with the fact that his marriage was now over. Even if he'd wanted to, he knew there was no forgetting, no making this better.

Markus briefly collapsed over the back of his wife, blanketing her body with his own heat as he tried to squeeze out one final moment of intimacy before hardening his heart once again. For his own sanity, he needed to reclaim the blinding anger he'd felt since discovering her betrayal. He wanted to hate her, but her continued soft cries for forgiveness were starting to sway him. He needed to get the hell out of there before he did something really stupid.

Not in a million years would he have ever thought he could walk out and leave his wife in a place like The Punishment Pit. His pain and regret were palpable, but the anger he'd felt had left him with the cum he shot deep inside her. All that was left was his grief over losing the woman he loved.

Why can't I hate her? It would make walking away so much easier.

As if they'd choreographed the scene ahead of time, his best friend came bursting into their private box just as Markus was standing upright, pulling his cock out of his wife's dripping wet pussy. Brianna was still lost in her own little world of post-coital recovery and couldn't see the meaningful look shared between the two men.

Markus didn't even try to hide his broken heart from his dominant friend. He took a minute to get his emotions under control, wiping his tears away on his shirtsleeve as he steeled himself to be strong once again.

Markus's heart was racing as the moment of decision had arrived. Even as he'd arranged to bring Bri to the club, he truly hadn't known if he'd be able to go through with leaving her here. The thought of her being punished like the submissive he'd just witnessed turned his stomach. If only he could forgive her, but he knew it was too late for that now. He could never trust her again. Markus reluctantly nodded and with that simple, defeated nod of his head, Lukus's face turned steely.

With a final supportive glance at Markus, Lukus marched to Brianna and yanked her to her feet by her long, thick hair with his left hand as his right clutched her breast. Brianna was forced to face the two men. Terror took over as she realized it was no longer her husband touching her. Her knees buckled again and only Lukus's support kept her standing.

Markus took a step back. Protecting her was no longer his job.

When Lukus finally spoke, his voice was laced with venom. "So, you're the selfish whore who cheated on my friend Markus. I can't say that I'm pleased to meet you considering the circumstances, Brianna."

Her watery eyes widened with recognition. "Oh God, you're Markus's old college friend?" Markus could see his wife putting the pieces of the puzzle together.

A menacing smile came to Lukus's face. He looked like a man who was ready to go to battle for Markus and Brianna was his target. His friend's eyes never left Brianna as he spoke to him. "Markus, I'm glad you got one final punishment fuck in before you cut this worthless whore loose. You, bitch, get on your knees and suck your husband's dick clean one last time. The entire time you're on your knees, I want you to think about how you had it all and you threw it away."

Both Brianna and Markus stood frozen until Lukus shoved her to her knees, wrapping his hand behind her head and pushing her face forward as Markus slid his dick into his wife's mouth. He was no longer hard so she was able to fit most of his tool into her mouth, but as she continued to suck his cock clean, he could feel himself getting hard again. He hated that he still felt any measure of physical attraction to her in spite of her infidelity. Pulling away and tucking his prick back into his slacks, he tried to think of the best thing he could say to destroy his wife the way she'd shattered him.

"No need to blow me, Brianna. I need to save a little juice for the woman I plan on picking up and taking home to fuck in our bed tonight. While you're here getting punished by my friends, I'm gonna go home, get drunk, and fuck an endless string of whores just like you until it doesn't hurt anymore."

The devastated look on his wife's face confirmed his words were a direct hit. Markus worked to hide the sense of revulsion he felt at what he'd just said.

As his words started to sink in, Brianna once again reached out from her kneeling position to grab onto Markus's legs like she was holding on for dear life. "Oh, my God. You can't leave me here Markus. Please... I'm so sorry. I love you so much. I'm begging you. Please let me come home with you and we can fight this out together. Don't give up on us, yet. I'll make it up to you, I swear."

Markus felt like he was going to be physically sick. He roughly pushed Brianna back, stumbling away, out of her reach. Lukus had to step in and restrain her as she wildly fought to leave with him.

His friend's voice was soft and sympathetic as he spoke. "Go home, Markus. You brought her here for a reason. Let me do my job. I got this."

Markus hesitated.

Can I do this? Can I walk away and leave her here?

He forced himself to picture his beloved wife getting fucked by her ex-boyfriend and he had his answer. She'd made her choices and now she was going to live with them. He was shaking with emotion as he made eye contact with his friend.

"Lukus," was all he could manage to say around the lump in his throat before looking down at his wife. "Goodbye, Brianna. I really did love you."

He turned and left without a backward glance.

CHAPTER TEN

BRIANNA

Brianna's heart was breaking. Witnessing Markus's pain was her final undoing. The fact that he could walk out and leave her here told her that she had truly lost him. She knew she should have been afraid of what was to come, but on another level, she welcomed the pain she knew she was about to receive. She deserved it.

She slowly looked up until her gaze fell upon the haunting, dark eyes of her captor.

"I have some really bad news for you, sweetheart," he said. "Markus is my friend—a very dear friend and I owe him big time. Here's how this is gonna go. I'm gonna take you down to the stage. And once we're there, I'm gonna make you wish you'd never been born."

When Brianna refused to break his gaze, his grim scowl turned into an evil smile.

"I see. You think I'm bluffing? You don't believe me?"

After several more seconds of their showdown, Brianna finally answered. "Oh, I believe you, I just don't care. I deserve everything you're going to give me and more. You're right. I had it all, and I threw it away. If I've lost Markus, then there's nothing you can do that will hurt worse than that." She continued to stare at him defiantly when it hit her. "How ironic that only now do I finally get to meet the infamous, Lukus, the one Markus worked so hard to help in court."

Her husband's friend smirked. "Now you understand just how much I owe him. The ironic thing is tonight was meant to be a celebration for me, Derek, and Markus. Instead, you had to go and let someone stick his dick in you and break my friend's heart. I almost feel sorry for you, Brianna. I'm not the kind of man you want to make angry. But I'm furious, and this is personal. You hurt my friend. I'm going to hurt you... bad."

His words were a direct hit, collapsing her legs from under her. He grabbed her in time to keep her from tipping over just before picking her up and moving into motion.

Brianna's trip from the balcony to the stage occurred in a haze of numbness and fear. She was carried over the shoulder of her husband's friend, only vaguely aware of Lukus stopping to feed his security code into keypads as they passed through several locked doors.

She suspected she should be struggling to get away. For a moment she had the ridiculous hope of calling for help. But her cell phone was in the car, and even if she had it, who would she call? Her brother? Her parents? She couldn't imagine facing them with the shame of what she'd done.

What about Tiffany? Under normal circumstances, the answer would have been an unequivocal yes, but tonight Brianna wasn't so sure. Hadn't Tiffany warned Brianna repeatedly that she was playing with fire? Her refusal to call the police when Jake had arrived at the shop and the resulting repeat infidelity caused friction between the best friends.

God, I wish I'd listened to her. Blackmail or not, whatever happens now, I deserve it.

The dance music was much louder in the club again when Lukus finally stopped walking and unceremoniously dumped Brianna on her ass. She was horrified by what she saw. They were backstage, but the area was a replica of the same dungeon on the stage, with a few extras.

She was struck again by the reality of her situation. This was no theater. There were no porn stars waiting to go on-stage to perform. There was no make-up or dressing rooms. This club was one big punishment dungeon. And it was here she would be made to pay for her sins.

Three waist-high metal cages lined the wall. They looked like large dog kennels to Brianna—only at The Punishment Pit they were clearly used to lock up submissives. One of the cages was occupied by a girl tied in a way that had her pussy and ass sticking out of a two-by-two hole in the cage. The lewd display had an obvious, depraved logic; with her bottom so presented, the girl's Master could punish or fuck her at his whim.

Bri had been too entranced by the sights around her to notice that Derek had joined them backstage. He was squatting down right in front of Brianna, sizing her up. "You're the fucking bitch who was stupid enough to cheat on Markus. You must really have shit for brains. I'd be saying my prayers now if I were you."

Brianna remained silent. What was there to say? She had no idea how Markus found out about Jake, but now that he knew, it seemed pointless to fight.

Derek moved to stand beside Lukus. They spent a few minutes huddled together, talking too quietly for her to make out what they were saying.

As she was straining to listen, she glanced across the room near the door to the stage. Kneeling quietly near the door was the slave girl who had been on stage at Lukus's feet. The girl's eyes were obediently lowered, but as Brianna watched her closely, she shot Bri what might be interpreted as a reassuring smile. It was the first bit of comfort Bri had felt since entering the building.

The men stopped talking and returned to Bri. Lukus squatted down at eye level, and when she failed to look at him, he reached out and almost tenderly placed his hand under her chin, raising her face up to meet his steely gaze. They sized each other up for a few seconds before he laid out what was about to happen. "Just for the record, you should know I don't agree with the course of action Markus has asked me to take with you tonight, Brianna. Personally, I'd like to take you out there and spend the next three days putting you through every conceivable punishment my sick mind can think up. Unfortunately, I can't because you aren't a member of the club and Markus wants to protect Derek and me. Here's how this is gonna work. I'm going to drag your ass out to center stage and string you up to the whipping post. Then I'm going to lay out your crimes along with all of the evidence against you. You're then going to be given a choice of signing one of two pieces of paper. Personally, I'd love to force you to sign them both, but Markus has made it clear to me I only need you to sign one."

He stopped long enough to make sure Bri was still paying attention before continuing on. "The first piece of paper is a standard contract that all members sign when they join The Punishment Pit. It outlines the rules of the club and grants legal consent for Master Derek and me to punish members in any way we deem appropriate, for as long as we feel appropriate. Every member is given a safeword, which they can invoke at any time, and when they do, the punishment stops while we evaluate. If their life is not threatened and I think they're just trying to escape, the punishment continues until I say it's done. We don't play games here. Of course, we can't force members to stay. They can resign their membership if they disagree with my decision."

Brianna felt a surge of hope knowing they wouldn't touch her unless she signed a contract. She realized now that Markus was likely representing the club over some dispute with a member.

"Why would I knowingly sign a paper giving you legal permission to beat the shit out of me? Do you think I'm stupid?" Her voice was small even as she tried to sound brave.

"As much as I look forward to lighting up your ass, I honestly hope you don't sign my contract," Lukus replied. "I'd much rather you sign the second piece of paper—a letter of intent to proceed with an immediate, uncontested divorce. Markus is in pain and he just wants closure as quickly as possible. Against my advice, he's offering you one get-out-of-jail-free card to avoid your extended stay here at the Shangri-la. All you have to do is sign the intent to divorce papers and we cut you loose. You'll be out of our lives, and out of Markus's, for good. Hell, I'll even be a prince and let you use my cell phone to call someone to come pick you up."

As Brianna absorbed his words, she swore she could hear the pounding of her own heart. She knew she should have been grateful that she was being given any choice at all, but the realization that Markus had put into motion paperwork for a quick divorce in the space of just a few hours cut her to the core. Until Lukus said the 'D' word, she'd been holding out hope that Markus would cool down and possibly give her a chance to explain once she was punished.

Lukus didn't bother to wait for her answer. Instead he dragged Bri to her feet, sandwiching her between the two muscular men briefly before Derek grabbed her and threw her over his shoulder.

"Don't forget," Lukus told his partner as they headed to the stage. "If she chooses option one, she's all mine and then you'll have just one job tonight, Derek—to make sure I don't lose control and kill the bitch. I swear to God, I'm going to whip her raw." His words were menacing, but Bri suspected her husband's friend was just trying to scare her in an attempt to coerce her into signing the quickie divorce papers.

At least I pray that's what he's doing.

As they burst through the door to the stage, Brianna could feel the heat of the hot spotlights through her little black dress. She couldn't see the audience from her vantage point over Derek's shoulder, but she could tell the curtains must still be open because the club was quickly quieting down and the music was lowered.

Derek sauntered to the heavy whipping post and

unceremoniously dumped Bri from his shoulder. As she teetered on her heels, he reached up and pulled down manacles attached to a hook high on the whipping post. Fight or flight instincts told her to put up a fight, but his tattooed muscles flexing as he brought the chain lower convinced her fighting was futile. He locked each of Brianna's wrists into the heavy metal restraints, immobilizing her arms above her head.

When Bri realized she was facing the audience, she slammed her eyes closed, trying to shut out the horror of her situation. Testing her confinement, she conceded there would be no escape until the angry men allowed it.

Lukus paced the stage as he addressed the audience. "Members, tonight I have the unpleasant job of putting the wife of one of my oldest friends on trial for her infidelity to her husband. Tonight was supposed to be a celebration for her husband, Derek, and me. Instead I've been asked to make sure the little whore understands the severity of her *situation*." He moved over to her, so close now she could feel his warm breath as he leaned in to whisper in her ear. "You make your choice yet, sweetheart? You taking door number one or door number two?"

Bri refused to open her eyes as she answered in a voice loud enough for only her captor to hear. "Fuck you, Lukus. I'm not signing anything and you can't touch me or I'll sue your ass so fast, you won't know what hit you."

She could hear his sharp intake of breath followed by a slow, long exhale. The unexpected intimacy sent a shiver through her entire body, drawing a low laugh from Lukus. He stepped away from her and continued to address the club. "What Brianna here doesn't understand is that running the club is just my hobby. My *day job* is owning one of the most successful private investigation and security firms in the entire Chicagoland area."

She felt his glare on her as he continued.

"You thought you were being so careful, but several months ago Markus came to me to ask for my help. He didn't have anything concrete, but he just had a feeling that you'd cheated on him. See, he noticed what looked like faint cane or riding crop marks on your ass when you were in the shower and since he knew you didn't get them from him, he decided he might want to find out what the hell was going on."

With this new information, Brianna's eyes flew open. She saw Lukus smiling smugly at her. She'd been so careful and now to find out that Markus had seen the welts from her disastrous earlier tryst was alarming.

Sensing her disbelief, Lukus addressed her directly again. "That's right, bitch. Your husband had started to suspect things months ago. I really do have to hand it to you. We'd pretty much given up tailing you because you'd managed to keep yourself clean. We didn't trace any calls between you and any another man. We didn't see you meeting anyone. There were no suspicious charges on your credit cards. All in all, you looked to be the perfect, doting wife. Until today that is."

He had moved close to her again. "For the record, if you would have stayed within a few miles of your salon, you'd have most likely gotten away with your little fuck-fest, but since you were stupid enough to drive in your GPS-enabled SUV all the way to downtown Chicago and park at a big downtown hotel, you set off a few monitoring alarm bells. It took us all of ten minutes to pull security shots from your salon and see your ex, Jake, there to collect you for your afternoon booty-call. Add to that our tracking of your cell location as well as Jake's cell location and we have a pretty concrete case. But just in case you're going to try to convince me that you just went to the hotel to talk or something innocent like, say, exchange recipes, you should also know that once we decided we needed to know more about your location and activities, we enabled the recording device that my team installed in your big ol' purse months ago."

Lukus was in her face now, shouting at her. "Do you know what the hell it was like to sit next to Markus while we listened to your ex-boyfriend fucking you? That's right. Your purse was close enough to the action that we could pick up on every single nasty little detail. We could hear grunting through your orgasms when his cock was shoved in your traitorous cunt and then your ass. Those things were bad enough, Brianna... but you should have seen the look on Markus's face when he realized that you were actually enjoying being tied down... being spanked on your bare ass... even going wild when that asshole whipped you with his belt over and over."

Oh my God... Markus was listening the entire time. He's never going to forgive me. Never.

Finally, unable to control his anger another minute, Lukus grabbed a handful of Brianna's long hair and whipped her head back, leaning in over her to stare down into her tear-filled eyes. "What's it going to be, Brianna? Are you joining the club tonight or becoming a divorcee?"

She was trapped. She only had one choice that gave her even the tiniest chance of getting Markus to forgive her. With silent tears streaming down her face, Brianna answered his question. "I don't expect you to understand, but I love Markus. I will never sign anything that makes it easier for him to get rid of me. I'm going to do everything I can to prove to him how sorry I am and how much I love him so I'll never —do you hear me?—*never* sign the divorce papers."

"Well that only leaves the other, doesn't it?" Lukus asked, his voice deceptively soft. "I hope you know what you're doing, little girl. You may think you can handle the punishment because you get all juicy when your jerk-of–an-ex spanks your ass for a few minutes. But you have absolutely no idea what I'm capable of when it comes to dishing out pain. Last chance."

"I said never. I don't care what you do to me, Lukus. I'll never sign the divorce papers. I admit, I made the biggest mistake of my life six months ago, but I was only trying to fix it today. He's blackmailing me!" Bri was proud of how strong her voice sounded considering the rest of her body was crumbling. She could feel the manacles cutting into her wrists as her legs deflated under her.

"Blackmail? You expect me to believe that after listening to you coming again and again? You wanted what he was dishing out, admit it. Get the pen and contract, Derek," he ordered, his eyes still locked on Brianna's.

Lukus reached up and unlocked Brianna's right arm from her overhead lock, which only put more weight on her left wrist.

While Lukus waited for the contract and pen to arrive, he reached out and ripped the beautiful diamond necklace right off Brianna's neck. The clasp was strong, and the powerful yank lightly broke the skin at the back of her neck. As he worked to take her earrings and bracelet off, he let the club members know the significance of the jewelry.

"Did you enjoy wearing all these diamonds tonight?" he asked in a taunting tone. "Do you have any idea how lucky you were to have a husband who buys you expensive jewelry like this on your anniversaries?"

Derek was back and placing a pen in her free hand as he stood in front of her holding a thick packet of papers. He had flipped to the last page and she saw him pointing at the signature line. She looked up to meet Lukus's hard stare.

"What? I don't get a chance to review the details before I sign?"

His eyes narrowed as if to warn her she was only making things worse for herself. She finally broke the stare and, knowing she was defeated, signed her name on the document.

The second she was finished, Lukus ripped the pen out of her hand and yanked her arm up to re-attach the manacle until she began to feel it again cutting into her wrists.

"Now it's time to set your safeword," he said. "Remember, just like every other member, you can invoke your safeword, but the minute you do is the very minute I'm going to give you a pen and you're going to sign the divorce papers. You got that?" When she didn't respond, he chuckled. "I'm assigning you an easy-to-remember safeword—*divorce*—since that's exactly what you'll be choosing should you use it."

Her brain knew what the men were doing wasn't legal. She could sue them—call the police when she finally got free. Yet, she'd gladly go through hell for a sliver of a chance at Markus's forgiveness.

Derek returned with a large pair of sheers. For just a second he stood in front of Bri, letting her worry about what he had planned for the sharp implement. He started at the hem of her little black dress and proceeded to cut it off her body. Seconds later her bra joined her dress on the floor, leaving her standing against the whipping post in just her stockings and high-heeled shoes.

She was grateful the bright lights prevented her from seeing the audience; it was bad enough knowing they were out there, but to see them ogling her would have been almost unbearable. Then it hit her. Could Markus still be here? Did he stay to find out if she chose to take her punishment or sign the divorce papers?

She was thinking of Markus watching from their private box when they turned her to face the whipping post, and a moment later she felt the first sting of the bullwhip on her back. It wasn't unexpected, but the first lash still took her breath away. Her surprise turned to raw fear when the pain of the welt grew to a deep burn. As she wrestled with the discomfort, she heard the swish of the whip in the air and then felt the searing pain of the leather marking her again, this time lower, across her ass.

She managed to absorb only four lashes before she let the sobs begin to wrack her. Lash after lash, Lukus was ruthless, only taking twenty or thirty seconds between strokes. By the seventh lash Brianna began to scream for her husband. "Markus! Please, I'm so sorry! Markus help me! Please..." As her legs were not restrained, she attempted to move away, but the manacles secured her too tight to escape the fire of the whip.

There was no rescue for Brianna. She lost count

of the lashes somewhere around the fifteenth blow. She welcomed the pain as each stripe continued to pummel her back, ass, and legs. It was the strong medicine she needed to douse the blanket of guilt for hurting the man she loved.

As much as she blamed Jake for her disastrous day, she accepted the pain and punishment for her stupidity and weakness six months before. Her infidelity had set this debacle into motion, and she had no one to blame but herself for that.

Lukus only stopped when Brianna collapsed against the post, placing all of her weight on her manacled wrists. A line of warm wetness dripped down her raised arm and she heard him curse when he realized her right wrist was bleeding from where the metal had cut into her skin.

Bri was vaguely aware of Lukus removing the restraints. When she began to collapse to the floor, he scooped her up into his arms and for the tiniest of moments held her bare body against his muscular chest. While his touch on her striped skin renewed her anguish, the contact was also strangely comforting.

Lukus didn't say a word as he carried her to a spanking bench, gently placing her face down on the padded surface, stooping to secure each leg. Only after wrapping the abrasions on her right wrist in gauze did he strap her arms down tightly. Once the final waist strap had her completely immobilized, Lukus leaned close to her ear.

"Are you ready to sign your name again yet, Brianna?"

Her answer was weak but clear. "I told you. I'll never sign, Lukus."

"Suit yourself. We've only just begun. You have no chance of surviving without begging me to bring you the divorce papers. I'll keep punishing you as long as I need to. Save yourself some pain and embarrassment. If you stay here, I'm not just gonna do torturous things to your body. I'm going to enjoy debasing you, humiliating you in ways your naughty little brain hasn't even dreamed of before."

She was unprepared for Lukus to reach down and stroke the folds of her pussy. She was mortified when she felt how his fingers slid easily through her copious juices. Bri hadn't been consciously aware of her body's reaction to her punishment at the whipping post, but there was no hiding the fact that she was soaking wet.

Bri heard Lukus's whispered, "Jesus Christ," before he finally moved away from her, taking his probing fingers with him. Derek had moved in front of Brianna and was wedging a horrible, uncomfortable neck brace under her chin that forced her to hold her head at an angle allowing the audience to see every emotion crossing her tear-stained face. He then turned the spanking bench ninety degrees so that Brianna was squarely facing the audience. There would be no hiding for her during the next phase of her punishment. She slammed her eyes closed to try to shut them out.

Lukus wasted no more time talking. Brianna couldn't see what implement of torture he had chosen, but after the first three strikes against her striped ass, she was pretty sure he was using a wide leather strap, judging by the feel and coverage.

The fresh agony had Brianna struggling hard against her restraints as she wailed in pain. While the first hard slaps left her ass burning, it was clear to anyone watching Brianna that the real fire had begun to migrate to another part of her body. To her incredible shame, painful screams had been replaced with feral moans of sexual desire.

God, I hate that I need this. Please, Markus, forgive me.

Lukus

Lukus watched in amazement as he continued to dish out a full-force strapping to Brianna's already thoroughly punished ass. In his anger, he was holding nothing back, which made the scene playing out before his eyes even more unbelievable. He, better than anyone else in attendance, knew exactly what was happening as he heard Brianna's screams replaced by throaty groans. He switched angles and could see her pussy dripping with evidence of her arousal. With each vicious stroke he delivered, Brianna clenched her pussy in a feeble attempt to come.

Lukus was the Master's Master. Even back when he and Markus were roommates in college, he already knew he'd always live at the darker end of the sexual continuum. He enjoyed the fact that he'd managed to make a living specializing in the delivery of pain and humiliation to willing and naughty submissives. There was very little in the line of deviant sexual experiences that he hadn't witnessed first-hand. In his line of work, what was happening to his captive on stage was actually quite common. Still, it was completely unexpected from the wife of his old friend.

He continued to deliver the hard strapping at a steady rhythm, never allowing Brianna even a slight break to try and regain her composure. She was both crying out in pain and groaning in pleasure as he pushed her, harder and ever closer to the destination he knew he was driving her to.

Under normal punishment circumstances, he'd actually be holding back to extend the sub's punishment. But tonight, he wanted to know—no, he *needed* to know the truth. It took almost five long minutes of non-stop strapping to her now beet-red ass and upper thighs before he finally pushed her over the cliff into a powerful orgasm. He watched as

Brianna succumbed to waves of pleasure without so much as a brush against her clit. She'd come hard from the pain alone.

Only now did Lukus realize his own discomfort from the tightness of his rock-hard cock straining against his jeans. There was no hiding his arousal from the club members and he briefly flirted with the idea of whipping his erection out and burying it deep in Brianna's pussy. He immediately put the idea out of his mind. Despite having what some might deem a twisted sense of morality, he knew he could never touch Markus's wife like that. He'd seen the pain on his friend's face as another man had fucked Brianna. He wasn't about to go there.

The irony of the situation was not lost on Lukus as he realized in the process of pushing Brianna to her limit, he may have pushed himself over his own line. It had been a long time since he'd felt this close to losing control of himself, and he was nearly overwhelmed by his need for release.

Glancing around the stage, he found Master Derek, also a hard-core sadist, was taking advantage of his wife and full-time sub, Rachel, to service his needs. His eyes lingered on the couple for a few moments as Rachel knelt in front of Derek as he face-fucked her throat. Even though Derek was more than happy to share Rachel with him, Lukus had no desire for sloppy seconds tonight. He headed backstage with plans to take his frustration out on one of the slaves-in-training instead.

As he walked by Derek, he instructed him to leave Brianna alone for now. "Just finish up with Kristen's punishment and then call it a night," he said. "Once the show is over, come backstage and I'll let you know what's next." Lukus didn't wait for a reply. He knew Derek would carry out his orders as soon as he finished shooting his cum down Rachel's throat.

Lukus headed straight to his office and slammed the door with a loud bang. He was wound tight, pacing wildly, trying to calm himself. This was not how he'd expected Brianna's punishment to go. When Markus asked for his help in making sure his wayward wife got what she deserved, he expected her to last less than half an hour before signing the divorce papers. This new turn of events changed everything. He was going to have to rethink his entire strategy if he was going to break Brianna.

But before he did that, Lukus was going to have to figure out some way to tell one of his oldest friends that he was beginning to understand, at least on one level, why his loving wife had been unfaithful. It may not absolve her of her guilt, but it did at least explain a possible motive. Lukus poured himself a drink and downed it in a gulp, hoping to take the edge off his nervousness so he could figure out the best way to tell Markus that his wife was a pain slut.

CHAPTER ELEVEN

MARKUS

Markus hadn't even tried to sleep. What was the point? Waking up would just bring with it the renewed pain of losing Brianna. At least fatigue dulled the pain.

Heavy metal rock music was pounding through the house, his silly attempt at filling the conspicuous emptiness with something, anything, that might keep his mind from hearing the torturous sound of Brianna moaning in ecstasy as she was fucked by another man.

Not just another man... *the* other man. The same ass-wipe who'd almost put her in the hospital before she'd wised up and kicked him to the curb years before. The same fucking man who'd made Brianna so afraid of rough play that Markus had been willing to walk away from the BDSM lifestyle he'd been living since college rather than risk scaring her away with the type of violence that had been part of her relationship with Jake.

Markus found it wasn't really that hard to turn his back on his old lifestyle to live the life of a gentle, loving husband. Until yesterday, he'd considered meeting his wife to be the best thing that had happened to him in his entire life.

He'd been on a destructive path before he met Bri. His first marriage had failed when his dominance over his submissive wife, Georgie, had gone too far. His immature and oversized ego combined with a penchant for punishment play made for less-than-stellar Dom—let alone husband—material. He'd love to blame Georgie for walking out, but truthfully, she'd done him a favor. He'd needed the wake-up call of her leaving to get his attention.

Then came Brianna. She was everything good to his bad. She was innocent and young and happy—a breath of fresh air into his dark and dangerous existence. He'd put her on a pedestal and would have given her the world if it were within his power. He'd vowed to make damn sure his dominance didn't ruin his second chance at love.

A fresh wave of grief at the thought of losing her washed over him, along with the irony of the situation. He'd married one woman who'd professed to be a submissive, but who eventually left him because he'd been too dominant for her. He'd happily given up the lifestyle when he found a woman who professed to need a gentle, loving relationship, and had ended up losing her because he'd been too fucking gentle.

An audible groan escaped as he leaned back in the leather chair and closed his eyes to try and stop the room from spinning. The nearly empty liquor glass shook precariously in his hand.

What a fucked-up mess.

For the hundredth time since he'd left his wayward wife behind at The Punishment Pit, he began replaying the last twenty-four hours over in his mind, trying valiantly to see the missed cue of why the love of his life had done the unthinkable. He prided himself on reading people, on seeing clues that others missed. It was part of what made him a good trial lawyer. Was he just not paying enough attention, or was Brianna just that good of a fucking liar?

It never ceased to amaze him just how quickly life could change. In twenty-four short hours he'd gone from the highest of highs to the lowest of lows and almost every emotion in between.

Yesterday had begun early with a good-luck suck from Brianna. Knowing she was the antithesis of a morning person, he'd been touched that she'd woke up early just to send him off to closing arguments with a smile on his face. Her early morning blowjob had been the best kind of start to his day.

Then the whole day had been too good to be true. He'd nailed his closing arguments. He'd known the second he was done speaking that they were gonna

LIVIA GRANT

win. It took the jury less than two hours to come back with their unanimous verdict in his favor. The entire day had been picture perfect, right up until he tried to reach Brianna to share his good news. She always answered his call—always.

Had Lukus not been with him, he might have been tempted to let it go, afraid of what he might find if he dug a bit. But his friend had read him like a book. Having already done a full background check on Brianna, Lukus was well aware of Markus's concerns the year before. He hadn't known Lukus's security team still had monitors on Brianna's movement, or that they would text their boss with damning news that would change his life forever.

Markus knew his friend meant well. And even now, he knew that it was best to know the truth, as fucked-up as the truth may be. But sitting here alone, drunk, and broken hearted, it was tempting to wish he could just forget, or had never known.

Don't be such a pussy, Lambert. You're clearly not husband material.

No, his marriage days were over to be sure. Lukus had the right idea. Don't get tied down. Fuck a different woman every night. Markus had a lifetime membership to The Punishment Pit. He'd surely be able to find willing submissives who wouldn't mind a no-strings-attached fuck when he was in the mood. He could help Lukus punish wayward slaves and take out his frustrations all in one.

Yes, he'd been a fool to think he could live

happily ever after with his beautiful wife. Hell, they'd even been talking about starting a family soon. He felt pain for the end of yet another dream, but told himself that maybe men like him didn't deserve to have it all.

Finally worn down by his own self-loathing, Markus stumbled to his feet, dropping the now empty glass on the carpeted floor. He tripped over the many broken items he vaguely remembered throwing a few hours earlier. The large mirror above the fireplace was shattered and he cursed in pain as his bare foot encountered a shard of Brianna's favorite vase.

He somehow navigated safely to the guest bath near the kitchen and found an old prescription bottle of Ambien in the medicine cabinet. More than anything, he needed to shut his brain down and turn off the memories, both good and bad. Ambien combined with the staggering amount of alcohol in his system should do the trick. He washed the tiny pill down with the last lukewarm swig from a beer he'd left in the bathroom earlier and stopped to take a whiz before returning to the great room. He collapsed facedown onto the leather sofa. Relief finally came in the form of a drug-induced sleep.

Lukus

I n spite of being stretched out in his comfortable king-size bed, Lukus suspected he wasn't getting much more sleep than his captive. After whipping Brianna to orgasm the night before, he'd stormed back to his office just in time. He'd nearly lost control on stage—something that had never happened in the over five years since he'd opened the private sex club. It had taken all of his willpower to turn away from his friend's wife without releasing his oversized cock and plunging it into her dripping wet pussy.

He rolled to his back with a groan, trying to make sense of the situation. Lukus had always prided himself on his control—control over the submissives of the club and even their Doms at the club, control over his successful security business, control over every woman he'd ever been with. Hell, he was even a pro at self-discipline, a skill that had served him well. He took pride in being able to control his own emotions, never letting them get in the way when punishing wayward slaves, or protecting people and places guarded by his elite security team.

The confusion he felt now was unsettling, even if he did understand the root cause. For the first time in what felt like forever, Lukus felt guilty. He'd never coerced anyone to join The Punishment Pit before, but that was exactly what he'd done to Brianna last night. He'd blackmailed her. He'd physically and mentally scared her until he'd broken her will, and it was not sitting well with him.

The irony of the timing was not lost on Lukus. Just yesterday he'd been acquitted of physically forcing two former club subs into degrading and humiliating acts. Throughout the nearly year-long legal ordeal, Lukus had never once felt guilty. He'd done nothing wrong with the two women in question. They were adults who had joined the club with their full-time Doms and had been given the complete details of what membership would entail. For months, they'd enjoyed watching other reluctant subs being punished, but only when it was their turn to be center stage had they called the police, claiming sexual battery and assault.

Markus had helped him draft the club's membership contract years before, so he was the perfect lawyer to defend his friends when they found themselves facing charges. Lukus had never doubted his innocence, or Markus's ability to get them acquitted. Markus had quickly gotten the criminal charges dropped and then yesterday had gotten Lukus and Derek a no fault, zero damages verdict on the civil charges.

Now, not even twenty-four hours later, Lukus felt the weight of guilt that came from knowing that he'd truly crossed the ethical line he'd been trying to straddle his entire professional life. But, worse, he also knew he needed to push these emotions down deep. His loyalty had to be to his friend, Markus. He couldn't let the guilt over how he'd coerced Brianna into signing the contract change anything. His friend wanted a quick divorce so he could put his wife's betrayal behind him. Lukus's job was clear. He'd promised to get Markus a quick, uncontested divorce and that was what he intended to do.

His resolve fortified, Lukus began to plot out how he was going to break Brianna. For all their sakes, he knew the faster she signed the divorce papers, the better off they'd all be. He'd planned on using traditional punishment techniques like spanking, paddling, bondage, and whipping, but now that he knew those punishments would actually turn her on, he had to change strategy.

As much as he dreaded it, he knew the next best way to punish someone like Brianna was to layer in humiliation punishments. While humiliation tactics were not what he would ordinarily choose for his friend's wife, he was going to have to head that direction if he hoped to wrap things up with Brianna quickly. He reminded himself that she had put this into motion by letting her ex-boyfriend fuck her so he really shouldn't feel any guilt. She had it coming.

Yeah, right. You keep telling yourself that, sport.

Still, he had to wonder why she'd done it. Had it truly just been her craving for pain? Before meeting her, he'd thought Brianna was just a gold-digging bitch after Markus's money. After watching her carefully last night, his sixth sense told him it wasn't that simple. Lukus remembered that after Markus's first marriage ended in divorce, his friend had denounced the BDSM lifestyle he'd been living and purposefully married Brianna, someone outside of their circle.

Lukus had tried not to take it personally that Markus kept him and the entire BDSM lifestyle hidden from his new wife. Considering how close the two men had been since college, it still seemed ridiculous that Lukus had never met Brianna until last night. He had to chuckle at the irony of Markus being unaware that the wife he'd worked to protect from his BDSM past was, in fact, a closet submissive.

He glanced at the alarm clock on the night table. Only 5:20am. Way too early to get up. He needed to get some rest. After tossing and turning, Lukus eventually drifted off into a restless sleep.

When Lukus awoke a short hour later, it hit him—the perfect plan to move Brianna closer to signing the divorce papers as quickly as possible. He wasn't sure why he hadn't thought of it earlier. It was still early on a Saturday morning, but after a few minutes of plotting, he reached for his cell phone to make a call to put things into motion.

He scrolled through his many contacts until he found the number for Dr. James Chambers. Hitting *CALL* he sat upright on the side of the bed, his morning hard-on jutting out from his muscular body.

The call was just about to rollover to voicemail when he heard his friend answer. "Lukus, you better have a damn good reason to be calling me before seven on a Saturday morning."

Lukus chuckled. "I missed you, too, James."

"Fuck you. You know I've never been a morning person, and this is my day to sleep in. You'd better be at the hospital about to bleed out if you're calling this early."

Lukus could hear a woman's sleepy voice in the background. "Who is it, sir?"

"It's just Master Lukus. Go back to sleep, baby. You should be able to get another hour in before the kids wake up," his friend answered.

For Lukus, the short conversation between husband and wife provided a glimpse into his old friend's happy marriage. The lucky bastard had found himself the perfect submissive while they were still in college. While Markus and Lukus had been having fun playing the field and experimenting with increasingly aggressive sexual encounters, James had been smart enough to propose to Mary right after graduation, recognizing he'd found a diamond in the rough.

She'd proven to be a strong woman, helping to put her husband through medical school and was now raising their two sons while managing to still live as the perfect submissive in private. Their marriage was not just a typical D/s relationship, although they loved to play the whole erotic Master/slave games as much as anyone else who belonged to the club. No, their relationship had another more intimate, deeper layer.

James and Mary also practiced domestic discipline in their marriage. James was the head of their household and Mary deferred to him for all major decisions. On the rare occasion she disobeyed, her husband disciplined her with a spanking. They rarely came to The Punishment Pit these days, but Lukus always knew Mary had done something really naughty when James would bring her in for a punishment session with Lukus. His morning hard-on got even harder thinking about the last time he'd been able to paddle Mary's plump ass to a nice rosy red.

Lukus had been subconsciously trying to find his own *Mary* for years. The more time passed, the more he'd come to appreciate how very rare it was to find the perfect mix of strength and submission in a woman. He saw his share of submissive wannabes, but when tested, they were only half committed.

Then there were the all-out submissives who were one hundred percent committed to the BDSM lifestyle. He used to think that was the type of woman he needed to make him happy, but after several failed relationships with full-time submissives, Lukus had to reluctantly acknowledge that he was bored by women who never challenged him.

Finding a woman who could master that delicate

balance of strength and submission had begun to feel like his own personal mission impossible.

"Tell Mary I'm sorry for waking her," Lukus told his friend. "And let me remind you again what a lucky bastard you are to have her snuggled up next to you. When we hang up, I'm gonna be jacking off my morning woody and you can roll over and get a good-morning fuck from your perfect sub." He tried not to sound as jealous as he felt.

"Did you really call me at this ungodly hour to talk about morning hard-ons? Now that you mention it, I have just enough time to roll my wife over and take her hard before the kids wake up, so why don't you spit it out so I can hang up?" Lukus could hear his friend's chuckle as well as a squeal from Mary.

Lukus took a deep breath before asking his favor. "I need your help this morning. Can you come into the club with your bag of goodies?"

"Sorry, but I don't have time to come and play doctor today, Lukus. The boys have a soccer game around eleven that I need to be at. They're in the playoffs."

"James, the soccer dad. Who'd have thought you'd turn into the model husband and father after living the life of the deviant doctor for so many years?" Lukus knew how to push his friend's buttons. He knew that as happy as James was, he was still feeling self-conscious about being tamed by his family life.

"Hey, you can give me all the grief you want. I

know you'd give your right nut about now for your own family. So cut the shit, Lukus. What's this really about?" James had always been one of the few people who could keep Lukus honest.

"It's Markus. He needs our help. His wife cheated on him and she's here. He wants my help in getting her to see the error of her ways."

"Brianna? No way. We've gone out to dinner with them a few times. There's no way she cheated on Markus. She doted on him all night long."

Fuck. This complicates things.

He should have suspected that James might have already met Brianna. Lukus pushed down the bitterness of the years of distance there'd been wedged between him and Markus, focusing instead on his current mission. It was especially hard to admit that Markus had introduced his wife to all of their friends.

Except me.

He spent a few minutes stepping through all that had happened the day before with James, repeating his request for his old friend's help.

A pregnant pause was finally broken by a sigh from James. "I don't know, Lukus. I like Brianna. I don't like the idea of humiliating her like this. It pisses me off if she really did cheat on him and she does deserve to be punished, but Markus should be handling this himself."

"Even if I don't disagree, I'm determined to help Markus. You've brought Mary here for punishments plenty of times. What's the difference?"

James's tone was growing impatient. "If you're asking me to bring my bag of goodies, this is different, and you damn well know it."

"Okay, okay... maybe you're right. Regardless, I still need your help. Will you come? For Markus?"

There was silence on the line for a long minute. Lukus began to think they might have been disconnected when James finally answered. "Yeah, I'll come, but I don't like it. Are you sure Markus wants this?"

"Markus wants her to sign divorce papers and this is what it's gonna take to make that happen." Lukus's voice sounded stronger than he actually felt. He hoped he was right about how quickly this would bring an end to the dangerous game they were playing.

"Fine. I'm gonna make love to my wife and jump in the shower. I'll be there as soon as I can, but I can't stay long. I really do need to leave in time to make it to the soccer match."

"No problem. See you soon, doc."

After they disconnected, Lukus headed off to shower to get his day started. He wondered how Brianna fared in her cage overnight. He pushed down the guilt he felt for confining her alone in such a cramped space.

"Stop being such a pussy," he told his reflection.

"She deserves every devious thing your sick mind can dream up."

Lukus felt better as he headed to the shower. He'd much rather drag his friend's wife in to suck him off, but knowing that wasn't in the cards, he settled for stroking his soapy cock until thick ropes of cum splashed the shower tiles. Just thinking about how hot Brianna's body looked draped over the spanking bench the night before made him contemplate jacking off a second time in hopes he'd be able to contain himself when he saw her naked body again this morning.

CHAPTER TWELVE

BRIANNA

Brianna awoke with a start. She'd been having a nightmare. As she kept her eyes closed, trying to calm her racing heart, all she could remember was she'd been in trouble. She needed help desperately. As the fuzziness faded, unwanted details started to flood back.

An unidentified man had chased her into a large, dark room. Once there, she'd been relieved to see Markus on the other side, but no matter how hard she tried to move toward him, he kept moving away from her. She had tried calling out to him, but it was like he couldn't see or hear her. She was invisible to him. When Markus started passionately kissing a scantily clad woman, she'd jolted awake.

Bri stretched and both her arms and legs hit metal. The sickening realization dawned that her nightmare was real. She was curled up on a thin mat lining the bottom of a three-foot by three-foot metal cage, not big enough to stand, sit, or even stretch out. Unwanted memories flooded back, reminding her she was in the backstage dungeon of The Punishment Pit. Even worse, guilt for the reason why she was there crashed over her.

Stay calm.

There were no windows, making it impossible to tell what time of day it was. She could only guess it was either very late or really early, as the club was eerily quiet.

Hot anger at being left to sleep in a cage like an animal, a possession, burned inside until the events of the previous day couldn't be ignored. Her betrayal, her overwhelming guilt, Markus's deep anger, the heartbreaking pain in his eyes, his wanting a divorce, his abandonment of her, the humiliation of her punishment...

She vaguely remembered Derek carrying her backstage not long after Lukus had whipped her to her shameful orgasm on stage in front of everyone in the club. He'd forcibly shoved her into the cage, ignoring her as she'd begged to be allowed to call Tiffany. She'd waited what seemed like hours for Lukus to come check on her, but he never did. Finally, she'd fallen asleep.

Brianna gave in to the urge to cry. Bitter sobs wracked her sore body as she curled into a tight ball, shivering as cool air brushed over her naked body. Bri rolled slightly, attempting to see if there might have been a blanket or sheet in the cage to shelter her from

LIVIA GRANT

the chill. The second she rolled onto her back a sharp pain struck from her shoulders down to the back of her knees. All of the welts from Jake and her punishment at the hands of Lukus were still alive and well.

Time crawled by as she lay curled up in agony, unable to sleep. She was thirsty, a little hungry, and had to pee. The last time she'd gone to the bathroom was at Hugo's, and that seemed like a lifetime ago. She tried to feel sorry for herself, but each time she did, she thought of the pain in Markus's eyes and reminded herself that she deserved to be uncomfortable.

She couldn't stop thinking of her husband, at home in their bed right now. Was he curled up next to another woman as he said he would be? Did he pick up someone and take her home to their bed to fuck as revenge? The thought of her husband with another woman caused her more pain than the severe whipping she'd received the night before at the hands of Master Lukus. She took a minute to pray he hadn't meant what he said, and that he'd just been trying to hurt her like she'd hurt him.

I have to stay strong and find a way to convince him how sorry I am.

In the dark of the small cage, alone and afraid, Brianna swore she would spend the rest of her life making this up to Markus. She'd never allow another man to touch her again, and since she didn't want to spend the rest of her life alone, she just had to figure out how to make things right between them.

Unable to find a blanket in the dungeon's dim light, Brianna curled back up into a ball in an attempt to get warm, surrendering to sleep again and the vivid nightmares it brought.

B rianna's bladder was about to burst by the time she finally saw Lukus emerging from across the backstage area. She hated how calm he looked. He'd obviously had a shower; his dark hair was still damp. He'd skipped shaving and the rough, dark stubble on his handsome face gave him a dangerous, bad-boy look that caused her core to wake up and take note. She told herself that it was fear causing her body to react, but if she was honest, she had to admit she was drawn to Lukus's power, his strength.

Wake up Brianna! He's the enemy.

She didn't wait for him to get closer before she let him have it. "God damn you, Lukus! I can't believe you actually put me in a cage and left me here, naked and freezing, as if I'm a dog. I know Markus is angry with me, but I won't believe he actually condones you treating me like this."

He'd arrived next to her cage and squatted down to eye level with his reluctant captive. "Nice to see you this morning too, Brianna. If you wanted the deluxe accommodations, you should have kept your legs crossed. Whores who cheat on their husbands don't have much in the way of standing around here, sweetheart."

She hated how casual he sounded, especially when she was trying to keep from panicking. "What would have happened if the building caught on fire? I could have been trapped... killed. It's not safe to keep me locked up and unattended like this."

Lukus laughed out loud, catching her off guard. Until now, she hadn't seen him smile, let alone laugh. She hated how his face lit up. She was pretty sure she saw a hint of a dimple in his chin, making him suddenly seem younger and less menacing.

She wasn't fooled.

His voice was annoyingly warm when he replied. "I think the only fire you should be worried about, little girl, is the fire that's going to light up your ass during your next punishment session."

He wasn't moving to open the cage and Brianna was getting impatient. "You need to open the door and let me out. *Now*. I really have to go to the bathroom."

He watched her intently before answering, all traces of humor now gone. "Let's get this straight right now. I don't *have* to do anything and that includes opening this door. I know you didn't have time to review the membership contract you signed, but if you had, you'd know you're little more than a puppet. And I, my dear, am the puppet master. The sooner you accept that, the better off you'll be."

"I'm not some simpering submissive here to bow at your feet. You can't treat me like this."

"We'll see about that, won't we?" He stood and moved away from her.

Brianna panicked. "Wait! Lukus. Where are you going? I told you. I really need to go to the bathroom."

His dark green eyes were intense as they took her in. "Is that any way to ask your Master permission?"

She hated the slight smirk she saw playing on his lips, but she knew she needed to play nice. "Please," she said through gritted teeth.

"Please, what?"

"Please, open the door so I can go to the bathroom."

He stood staring at her, waiting expectantly, his muscular arms crossed over his broad chest.

She didn't know why he was just waiting. "What?"

"It's time you address me properly. I'm not 'Lukus' to you. You will call me either 'Master' or 'Sir.' Try again."

Bri's hackles were up. How dare he? Still, she feared she'd need to play along if she was ever going to get a chance to escape. Swallowing her pride, she managed to choke out her request again, this time hoping it met with his domineering approval. "Would you please open the door and let me out so I can go to the bathroom... *Sir*."

He made her wait for several long seconds before smiling and walking back to the cage. He detoured to pick up something from a nearby table. Brianna couldn't see what he had in his hands until he squatted near the door of her cage.

"Put your hands through the hole." His tone left no room for dissent.

Bri pushed her wrists through the small opening in the door, her request coupled with a reflexive, "Yes, Sir" before she could catch herself. She knew he was enjoying her submission because a sly smile lit up his face as he began locking fleece-lined cuffs around her outstretched wrists. She was grateful he didn't connect them together, leaving her more range of motion.

"Now your ankles," he demanded.

Brianna was not at all happy about this request since it required her to sit back on her sore, bruised bottom in order to stick out each ankle. The pain from sitting was sharp and an unwelcome pleasure washed through her as she remembered the strong punishment at Lukus's hands the previous night. A gasp escaped as she moved and she glanced up in the hope that Lukus hadn't heard.

He smiled at her. "How's your ass today?"

"You know exactly how it is, you bastard," she snapped without thinking.

He was just finishing locking the fleece-lined ankle restraint as he grabbed hold of her foot and squeezed with full strength. Brianna cried out in pain.

"Care to try that answer again, sweetheart?" His

voice was deceptively calm, and his green eyes showed just how close to danger Brianna was skating right now.

With tears in her eyes, she tried again. "My back, ass, and legs are really sore today... Sir."

He squeezed for a few more seconds before releasing her. "Better. We'll get you trained yet."

Seeming satisfied that all the restraints were attached, Lukus unlocked the padlock securing Brianna's cage and swung the door open. She was forced to crawl out on her hands and knees, and she was grateful when he helped her up, his almost gentle assistance a contradiction to his earlier treatment. Her cramped legs felt like spaghetti as he supported her until she steadied herself enough to walk.

Only the pressure on her over-full bladder hastened her along. "I really need a restroom." She remembered to throw in a soft "Sir" as an afterthought.

Lukus took her hand in his and steered her across the room to a corner of the dungeon she hadn't seen yet. She didn't see a door in this direction, which confused her. When Lukus stopped near the wall and dropped her hand, Bri looked up at him.

"Where's the door to the bathroom?" she asked, but when he raised an eyebrow, she quickly added another "Sir."

"Slaves don't have the privilege of a private restroom—or a real toilet for that matter."

Bri looked around and with horror knew immediately he intended her to squat over the five-gallon bucket sitting in the middle of what looked like a four-by-four tiled shower floor with a drain in the middle. There was even a showerhead jutting out from the wall just behind the bucket.

Her voice was barely a whisper. "You can't be serious?"

His voice was so powerful in contrast to her own. "Oh, I've never been more serious. If you need to pee, here's your bucket, or you could just squat over the drain."

She could feel him staring at her as she looked down at the bucket, her heart racing. They stood in a silent showdown until she finally looked up at him, tears streaming down her face. "Oh God, please. Don't make me do this. I can't."

His eyes bored into her. Already stripped naked, she didn't think she could feel more vulnerable in front of her captor, but she'd been wrong. The harsh look on his face was stripping another layer from her already fragile psyche.

"Well, I guess I could be persuaded to let you use my master bathroom upstairs. You could take a hot bath and use all of the facilities... privately, of course." He paused as she briefly got her hopes up. "All it will take is one little signature on your divorce papers. You sign and I take off the cuffs, get you a hot bath, a soft bed, and some clothes. I'll even let you call that liar-of-a-friend of yours and let her come pick you up. You can go on your merry way, free to start the rest of your life."

His words toughened her up. "I told you last night and I'll repeat it again because it seems you might have a hearing problem. I am never—do you hear me? —*never* going to sign the divorce papers." After a dramatic pause, she defiantly raised her chin, looking him square in the eye. "Sir."

He slowly broke into a smile that didn't quite reach his eyes. "Suit yourself. You have two minutes, then we're moving on."

Her bravery quickly evaporated as she realized the fragile position she was in. She was about to burst, but there was no way in hell she could squat over the bucket to pee —not in private and certainly not with him watching her. She made up her mind to just power through. "No, thank you. I don't need to go anymore, *Sir*."

"Okay. If you say so, sweetheart." He took her hand again in a deceivingly gentle manner and led her toward a door.

As they entered an office, the smell of coffee and pancakes jostled a growl out of her empty stomach. She glanced around, taking in the details of the homey, masculine space. The walls were lined from floor to ceiling with bookshelves holding hundreds of books. A comfortable-looking brown leather couch, comfortable-looking chair, and ottoman sat in the middle of the room.

A space between the shelves directly across from

his huge desk held high-tech entertainment equipment. Upon closer inspection, she also saw what appeared to be an opening to a small elevator.

"I live upstairs. I turned the top floor of the building into one huge loft."

Brianna tried to hide her surprise that he'd shared anything personal with her. Completing the room was a round, heavy wooden table with six padded chairs surrounding it. Decks of cards and stacks of poker chips were piled on the far side of the table and the scent of cigar smoke mingled with leather. It had the comforting, masculine scent of a man cave.

Lukus took a seat in front of the one and only plate of food placed on the table. Brianna pulled the chair out next to him, but he abruptly stopped her. "What the hell do you think you're doing?"

She was flustered. She truly didn't know what he expected of her. Suddenly more self-conscious than ever, she brought her arms up to cover her breasts and tried to hide her pussy from him.

"Do not sit at the table. You'll kneel here and I'll feed you what I think you deserve to eat." When she stood staring at him as if he was from outer space, he reinforced his point. "Kneel. Now."

He pointed to the floor and only then she saw the pillow placed there, presumably for her to kneel on. Their eyes locked in a heated stare down. Bri started out so very strong, but with each passing second of his probing gaze, she felt her resolve crumbling. She could feel the shivers beginning to shake her body and prayed that they were not visible enough for Lukus to notice. She didn't want him to know how deeply his dominance was getting to her.

He didn't need to say another word and it only took about thirty seconds before Bri's determination was gone and she found herself slowly dropping to her knees on the pillow. She couldn't bear to look him in the eye any longer, which was bad enough. She refused to let herself cry.

Be strong, if not for yourself, for Markus.

Lukus

Lukus was grateful Brianna finally looked down when she did. He needed some time to regain control over his own rambling emotions. He knew that had she continued to stare him down much longer, she would have seen his own hard edge wavering.

Why the hell am I letting her get to me?

Even though he didn't have a steady submissive at the moment, almost every weekend one of the club members requested a private punishment or training session with Master Lukus. He never had trouble being the strict disciplinarian they expected, having mastered hardening himself against a crying submissive. Their tears, and even screams, let him know he was getting his job done while feeding his own sadism. So how could a few quiet tears in the eyes of his friend's wife give him pause?

The answer was simple. It kept coming back to his guilt. Brianna was no ordinary club member. She had no clue what she'd been forced to sign up for, no idea of how dark his world could get. She couldn't fathom how severe a Master Lukus punishment could be and hadn't a hint of how much mind-blowing pleasure he could deliver to her hot, tight body.

Don't go there, dip shit.

His stomach churned with an uncomfortable roll as he thought about the devious, humiliating plans he had for his captive. He forced aside his doubts as he reached out to cut the pancakes and sausage on his plate. After taking a few bites, he poked the fork through a morsel and held it in front of Brianna. When she didn't open after a few moments, he ate it instead.

Lukus tried ignoring her as he grabbed his iPad, catching up on his email and current events while continuing to eat. Occasionally he stopped to offer her a bite, but she held firm in her refusal to eat from his hand.

When there were only a few bites left on his plate, he finally addressed her. "I'd think long and hard about refusing the next forkful I offer you, sweetheart, because I assure you, it will be the last food you're offered until much later today. I have big plans for you, and I suspect you might want to keep up your strength."

As she continued to hold her ground, defiance in her eyes, Lukus couldn't help but be proud of her strength. It'd been a long time since he'd met a woman like the one kneeling at his feet. Just his luck, she was completely off-limits.

There were only a few bites left when he held out the next offering of food for Brianna. Anger rolled off her, yet she closed her eyes and leaned forward, her mouth open. As she slowly chewed, Lukus reached to gently stroke the top of her head as he might a faithful family pet. As expected, she flashed him a defiant look and he was sure his ensuing chuckle fueled her anger. Regardless, he fed her the remaining three bites before handing her a cold bottle of water to wash down her breakfast.

She had to be thirsty, but she sipped the water sparingly, no doubt hoping to avoid compounding the pressure on her bladder. Piss play wasn't one of his favorite kinks but knowing it would only be a matter of time before Brianna lost the battle with her bladder turned him on nonetheless, not for the act itself, but the beautiful humiliation it would bring.

You really can be an asshole, Mitchell.

After setting the water bottle aside, his captive mustered the courage to demand answers. "What exactly is your plan? I already told you I'm not going to sign the divorce papers. Do you plan on tying me

173

up and wailing on my ass with every punishment tool you own until you have to finally give up?"

Their eyes found each other again and, for a brief moment, the showdown was amicable. Lukus then unmasked the deviant Master he'd been reining in, hoping to scare her into putting an end to their standoff.

"Brianna, I think it's time for you to learn there are an endless number of punishments at my disposal. Now that I know you actually get off on the pain of a well-delivered paddling, you've forced me to change my plan. I can't very well punish you with orgasms, now, can I?" He waited a minute to let that sink in before finishing his thought. "Sweetheart, I hate to tell you but there are way worse punishments than pain. I'm going to enjoy introducing you to a few of those this morning."

Lukus could tell his threat unnerved Brianna. Any other day, seeing a submissive begin to tremble with fear at his words would have him proud of his own mastery. Today, he just felt like an asshole. He was so distracted by Brianna, he'd failed to hear the light beep that should have alerted him to someone entering the club with their keycard. As a result, James's arrival startled him.

"What the hell is going on here, Lukus?"

Brianna and Lukus both swung around to see who'd entered. Lukus gave his friend a look that would intimidate a lesser man, but James simply shrugged it off.

Brianna, on the other hand, looked utterly confused at the appearance of the family friend. She raised her arms, attempting to cover her naked body. Lukus watched her closely and knew the second that her modesty took a backseat to self-preservation. He didn't stop her from jumping to her feet and rushing into James's arms, hugging him around his waist, holding onto him for dear life.

"Thank God you're here, James. You have to get me out of here. I need to get home to Markus. Did he send you for me?" she begged.

With her face buried against James's chest, Brianna was oblivious to the silent showdown the two dominant friends were having behind her back. If looks could kill, both men might have been dead on the floor. Lukus could tell James didn't approve of Brianna's naked and welted condition, but Lukus was just as furious that James was undoing all the progress he'd made that morning. Through dominance and humiliation, he'd been chipping away at her defenses, moving her closer to signing the divorce paperwork. Now, James was comforting her and setting them back.

James turned his attention back to the distressed woman in his arms, finally answering her. "Brianna, Markus didn't send me."

Bri hiccupped, brushing away some of her tears as she asked, "What do you mean he didn't send you? Why else would you be here?"

James glanced at Lukus and then back down at

Brianna. "Did you cheat on Markus?" When she didn't answer, he pressed the question. "Did you? Did you let someone else fuck you?"

Lukus couldn't see her face from his vantage point, but he heard the growing panic in her voice. "No... you can't be...?" Brianna shook her head in disbelief as she realized he'd not come to save her. Lukus knew her next question was laden with fear. "If Markus didn't send you, why are you here?"

Maybe this will turn out okay after all.

"I'm here because Lukus called me. I'm a member of the club, Brianna. Markus and I were roommates in college. You know that. What you may not have put together yet is that Lukus was our third roommate. Now, I'm still waiting for your answer. Did you let someone beside your husband fuck you?"

Brianna's head shook from side to side, her own brand of denial as she began to babble in her panic. "James... I didn't mean to. Please, you have to believe me. I love Markus so much. I never meant to hurt him. I should have told Markus when Jake tried blackmailing me. I can see that now." When James scowled harder, she continued on. "It was just a couple of times and I swear... I'd already realized what a mistake it was. I will never—*ever*—cheat on him again. I need to get home. I need to try to explain to him, try to make him understand..." Her rambling trailed off as she probably realized James's face was only growing redder with her explanation.

James grabbed her bicep, yanking her to him

roughly. "I think you're gonna have to help Lukus and me understand why you would shit on your marriage first and then let us decide if you have anything Markus might want to hear. And I'm going to warn you, I can't think of one possible reason that might be good enough to convince me that Markus shouldn't dump your ass. I have rather stringent rules when it comes to fidelity and I'm positive Markus shares those same values."

As she struggled to be free, Lukus caught a glimpse of her profile. Bri had the look of a deer caught in headlights, no doubt realizing that in the space of a few minutes she'd gone from having not one, but *two,* of her husband's dominant friends out to get her.

"I'm waiting," James demanded.

"You wouldn't understand." Her pitiful response came out as a whisper Lukus had to strain to hear.

"Try me." James was playing his role as hardass perfectly.

"It sounds terrible."

"Worse than hearing you let someone else fuck you?" James's voice was hard as nails and Lukus had the perfect vantage to see that his blue eyes had turned ice cold.

"Stop saying it like that," Brianna shouted in high-pitched panic.

James didn't give an inch, still gripping her arm to keep her from escaping his interrogation. "How would you like me to say it? I think calling it a fuck is better than saying you let someone else make love to you, isn't it? Or are you in love with someone else, Bri?"

"Oh my God, no! It's nothing like that," she shouted, and Lukus welcomed her panicked response.

I think we're making progress after all. We need to get this done, for all of our sakes.

"So, what was it like?" James wasn't backing down. His voice stayed firm as he pushed for answers.

"I don't need to explain myself to you! I need to talk to Markus. I'm begging you, James. Take me home to him." Brianna first reached to hold James's forearms, but when he didn't budge, she changed it up, grasping at his button-down shirt to pull him closer.

He'd sat on the sidelines long enough. Lukus moved to stand next to them. "Markus made it clear. He doesn't want to talk to you anymore. He won't believe a word that comes out of your mouth anyway. You fuck around and lie like a pro." Softening his voice slightly, Lukus tried again to convince her to take the easier way out. "There's no making this better, Brianna. The sooner you realize that, the sooner you can sign the paperwork and go on with your life."

Bri rounded on him. "I told you, Lukus," she hissed. "I'm not signing the damn papers. There's nothing you can do to me that will change my mind." The fire in her watery eyes was back.

The woman seriously had a death wish.

"We'll see about that, won't we?" he spat.

James stepped in between them. "Okay, that's enough you two. Brianna, I need to talk with Lukus privately."

Lukus wrenched Brianna from the relative haven of James's arms. "Come on, sweetheart. Let me get you settled in. Stay here, James. I'll be right back."

Her struggles to break free as he marched her out of the office were almost comical against his strength. With each step, he sensed her becoming more fearful. "Please... no. Don't put me back in the cage. I'm begging you. Don't make me go back in there, Lukus! I mean... Sir."

Ironically, she gave a sigh of relief when he walked her to the St. Andrew's cross. She clearly had no idea the levels of punishment he could deliver to her naked body once he had her immobilized and at his mercy.

If she had a clue, she wouldn't look so relieved.

Lukus positioned Brianna with her back against the wooden cross, snapping the rings on her wrist cuffs to a metal hook above her head. The only way she could keep her balance was to rise up slightly on her toes. He liked how the position left her completely vulnerable.

When he reached to secure the strap around her waist. For a moment, their eyes locked intimately, and her vulnerability made his breath hitch. Lukus tore his gaze away to break the dangerous connection he'd felt to his captive. Anger at his own emotional instability made his actions rough as he fastened the leather belt around her waist, making sure it was low enough to press on her already pressured bladder.

Brianna remained stoically silent as Lukus squatted to secure her ankles to the wide bottom of the crisscrossed wood. When he was done, he stared up at her naked body, assessing his work. Brianna hung painfully from her arms with only the cinched belt at her waist to provide support.

He should stand and move away. He should return to James before he did anything stupid. But his proximity to her bald pussy allowed him to catch a whiff of her musky core, freezing him to his spot. He was so close. It would be so easy to reach out to slide his fingers through the slick folds.

God damn it, Mitchell. Keep control, for Christ's sake. This isn't some sub here to play. She's Markus's wife and completely out of bounds.

Shaking his head to chase the temptation away, Lukus stepped away from her intoxicating scent before he did something stupid. He distracted himself by perusing the plethora of punishment devices on a nearby table as he tried to decide which implement was most likely to break Brianna's resolve.

His eyes met Brianna's as he headed back to the cross. It was easy to see the apprehension on her expressive face as she recognized what he held in his hands. She gasped as she watched him testing the tautness of the evil-looking nipple clamps on his own finger.

On autopilot, Lukus lunged forward to take Brianna's left nipple into his warm mouth. While his large hands cupped her heavy breasts, he began to suck her nipple hard, grazing his teeth across her tender body part. He'd intended to merely tweak her nipple to make a better target for the clamp, but once he got his first taste of her, he couldn't pull away any more than she could. His cock grew hard against the zipper of his jeans as he groaned.

Despite her own moan of pleasure, Brianna was the one who was finally strong enough to halt his insanity with a scream of warning. "Lukus, don't touch me like this. I'm still Markus's wife and you need to stop... *now!*"

Her words were like ice water, successfully waking him up to his own careless stupidity. Pulling his mouth away from her perfect C-cup breasts, he reached out and clamped on the viciously tight nipple clamp. Bri cried out from the sharp pain he knew was piercing through the tortured tip.

Deciding to use his hand instead of his mouth to perk her other tit, he pinched her right nipple until it was a nice, hard target for the second clamp. When he let the clamp snap shut, Brianna's panting erupted into a wailing scream for several seconds until the pain settled in, turning her scream to a guttural groan.

Lukus's cock grew impossibly hard as she screamed. He'd planned on finding some weights to attach to the chain hanging between her lush breasts, hoping to add to her discomfort. Instead, he decided his own discomfort necessitated a discreet departure. Without a backwards glance, he turned and headed back to duke it out with his friend, the devious doctor, leaving Brianna alone to wrestle with the pain in her arms, nipples, and bladder.

CHAPTER THIRTEEN

BRIANNA

Brianna was almost frantic by the time her husband's best friends emerged from the office. It seemed to her they'd been closeted in there forever, but without a clock, she couldn't tell, and the pain had made the minutes feel like hours. She was in agony and desperate for release, both from her restraints and her bladder.

Making things worse, her strapped and bruised ass was being pressed against the hard wood, sending renewed waves of heat through her weary body, resulting in confusing sensations of desire. The liquid heat gathering between her splayed legs was likely visible proof of her dilemma.

Bri waited anxiously for her captors to cross over and untie her, but when both men detoured toward the door to the stage without even so much as a glance her way, she lost it. Their faces had been hard... stormy. She prayed they were angry at each other, but she suspected their veiled rage was still directed squarely at her and that didn't bode well at all.

"I can't believe you left me like this!" she screamed out, trying to get their attention. "You two should be ashamed of yourselves. I know Markus doesn't know you're treating me like this. I demand you get me down now. Do you hear me? Lukus! James!" They were already out of sight before she shouted their names, leaving her to once again endure her pain alone.

Thankfully, it was only a few minutes before Lukus returned.

"Did you miss me, sweetheart?" His words may have been playful, but his tone was all business.

Pushing down her anger, Bri let her desperation show. "Please, Lukus. I'm begging you. Let me use your bathroom." Brianna swallowed hard, trying to keep from crying. She was shivering, both from the chilled room and from an excitement she could neither suppress nor explain.

"All in good time. We have a few other plans for you first." He was standing directly in front of her now, only inches away from her shivering body, close enough Brianna could feel the warmth of his clothed body and she hated how it comforted her. The seconds dragged on as they sized each other up. "Last chance, Brianna. I'm warning you—I'm gonna do whatever it takes to get you to sign those papers. It's what Markus wants, and I owe him that. You owe him that. Will you just sign them? Please?"

She was shocked that what started as a command had become a heartfelt request. His dark eyes were softening, almost pleading with her to acquiesce. Up until now, Bri had been obstinate in her refusal to sign. She was amazed Lukus seemed to have his defenses down. She took the small window of opportunity to try to get through to him with her pleas. "I told you Lukus. I'm never going to sign for a quick divorce. Please... I know you think you're helping Markus, but truly, I need to go home and talk to him. I need to tell him how much I love him and how sorry I am, how I plan to spend the rest of my life making this up to him. Please. I'm begging you. Give my marriage one more chance. Take me home."

For the briefest of moments, she thought he might have been listening, might have been ready to take her home and end the insanity—but it passed. She watched as Lukus hardened, transforming himself once again into the Master's Master.

Dragging his gaze away from her pleading eyes, Lukus made quick work of releasing first her ankles and waist before finally reaching up to unhook her wrists, allowing her feet to fully touch the ground. Her legs had fallen asleep and he had to catch her when she crumpled after being released from the cross. His hard cock pressed into her stomach as his arms held her steady and he stared into her eyes until

Brianna had to look away in an attempt hide the shameful desire she feared he'd see in them.

Lukus coldly pushed her away, stooping to grab her below the waist, and effortlessly lifting her to his shoulder in a fireman's hold. Brianna cried out from the sudden pressure on her full bladder and the sharp pulling on the chain linking her still-attached nipple clamps.

"You'd best hold it," he said. "I'll paddle you black and blue if you piss down my shirt, little girl."

"I think it will be better for our plan if we let her try the bucket again." James put his hand on Lukus's arm, stopping him. Brianna raised her eyes to the doctor's and they both knew that this time she wouldn't refuse to go.

Lukus paused to consider the suggestion before walking her to the bucket, dumping Brianna on her ass to the floor. She crawled to her knees and sighed with relief when both men did her the unexpected courtesy of turning away. Terrified they'd change their mind, she quickly crouched over the bucket and peed, her face flaming with embarrassment even though they weren't watching.

She barely had time to stand up before Lukus accosted her again. Over his shoulder Brianna went and she had no idea where she was until Lukus dropped her from his shoulder onto the edge of the gynecological exam table she'd seen from the audience the night before.

Manhandling her until she'd reclined back, he

wasted no time in securing her cuffed wrists at the head of the table. In her semi-seated position, Brianna would be able to see what was being done to her, even if she couldn't stop it.

James joined Lukus at the table and when each man grabbed an ankle, it was too late for Brianna to try and kick free. They made quick work of roughly pulling her legs high and wide—Lukus on one side and James the other as they secured her legs into the locking stirrups. These were unlike any stirrups found in a normal OB-GYN office—they were clearly meant to completely immobilize a 'patient' in the most vulnerable of positions.

As the men adjusted her legs to move her knees up even closer to her head, her ass and pussy were left completely open, at their mercy, ready for their viewing, touching, punishing, or—God forbid—even fucking. Things were clearly going from bad to worse and Bri fought back her panic.

Once she was locked in place, Lukus stepped away to lean against the nearby wall. His muscular arms crossed at his chest, he casually placed his left leg over his right at the ankle, lending the impression of a casual bystander. Brianna watched him closely as his eyes devoured her naked body. She didn't miss his quickened breathing, or the outline of his over-sized cock straining against his jeans. He shifted uncomfortably and a small thrill ran through her.

Serves his ass right for how he's treating me.

Lukus handed control over the scene to James

and it only took a moment for Brianna to realize he was playing the part of doctor in their sick game.

"Did you at least make your lover wear a condom when he fucked you?" James's tone was all business. Dr. Chambers was in session.

"He wasn't my lover; I told you that. But..." her voice trailed off.

"But what?"

"I get a birth control shot. I know he didn't get me pregnant."

"That's not what I asked you. Did he or did he not wear a condom? Did you let him shoot his cum into your body?" His voice was hard.

"He did."

"Which is it? Yes, he wore a condom, or yes, he shot his cum into your body?" James wasn't letting up.

Brianna's voice was reduced to a whisper. "He didn't wear a condom."

"Sounds like a really nice guy. I can see why you'd throw your marriage away for him." James's voice dripped with sarcasm.

His tone brought out her anger all over again. "What do you guys want from me? I know I was an idiot. Jake is a complete jerk and none of you are angrier with me than I am at myself for getting myself into this situation. If I could turn back time and never go with him, I would, but I can't."

James ignored her. He continued on as if she hadn't spoken. "Lukus tells me that Markus fucked you one last time before saying goodbye to you for good. I'm worried he might have been exposed to STIs. I'm going to get a blood sample from you and have it tested. Then I'm going to give you a full exam to see if there are any signs of sexually transmitted infections."

Brianna was humiliated. She felt like a whore, about to be poked and prodded because she might be diseased. She was sure that was exactly James's intent, and she was tempted to tell him 'mission accomplished' but held her tongue.

James took a small blood sample from her restrained arm. When Bri looked away from the needle, she saw Lukus watching her reaction carefully. His expression was unreadable.

As unpleasant as the blood draw was, things got worse when James settled on the stool at the end of the exam table. He wheeled himself close to her body and reached out with a gloved hand to begin his very personal examination of her body. At first, his touch was that of any reputable doctor, but within a few seconds his examination changed to that of a dominant Master. She felt his fingers roughly exploring her pussy, inside and out, as if he were gauging her response.

The unmistakable sound of Bri's rapid breathing mixed with the wet slurping sound of his probing fingers sliding up and down through her juicy folds. Her ass jerked up off the end of the table when his fingers grazed her clit. An unmistakable groan of pleasure escaped as he plunged what felt like two fingers deep into her core, expertly curling them to find her G-spot.

Desperation overwhelmed Bri when she realized she was nearly coming at the hands of someone other than her husband. She'd made a promise to herself while caged that she would never again let anyone other than her husband touch her sexually. Yet here she was just a few hours later, being forced to break her own promise.

Bri was shocked by her friend's boldness. Pushing her obvious pleasure aside, she issued the same warning to the doctor that she had to Lukus. "James, stop it right now. I'm still Markus's wife and I'm positive he doesn't want you doing this to me."

"That's where you're wrong, Brianna. I think Markus wants to know as much as possible about why you fucked around on him—why you'd risk everything for some jerk who treats you like shit. My examination will continue."

He reached down into a black bag at his feet and pulled out an abnormally large speculum. She could feel him rubbing the cold metal up and down the wet folds of her pussy before shoving it deep, drawing another groan from his captive patient. He roughly spread the device open, stretching Brianna's tender pussy, rendering her most private part public domain. Then he locked the device wide, causing painful cramps to wash through her lower body. He took his time reaching for a very long Q-tip to swab a sample from the walls of her cunt. Even after he secured her sample, he seemed to be in no hurry to relieve her discomfort. When she began to struggle, James smartly slapped the tender inside of her thigh.

Lukus spoke for the first time since the exam began. "I told you, sweetheart. You had your last chance. We're gonna do this our way now. Like I said, there are many ways to punish you that don't involve spanking or paddling. You're about to find out how very true my words were."

Brianna wasn't exactly sure what *their way* meant, but it couldn't be good. She barely paid attention as James finally removed the speculum.

Her next sensation was his touching her anus. Her eyes flew to James's as she saw the bottle of lube in his visible hand and felt his slick, gloved finger probing her tight hole. Brianna was too surprised to even complain when she felt him pressing a finger into her body, seating it up to the knuckle before circling his thick finger, bringing a strange sensation of fullness.

She was reluctantly forced to accept his finger caressing her rosebud and fought the urge to cry out as she was sore there. Bri closed her eyes, trying to regain control as she felt something hard being inserted into her ass. She opened her eyes just in time to see James hanging an enormous-looking enema bag on one of the high hooks of the rolling cart next to her. That was when she realized that James had just shoved an enema nozzle deep into her anus. In that moment she knew true panic.

"No! Please... not this... anything but this..." Brianna yanked against her restraints in a feeble attempt to free herself. She shook as she felt the invading fullness of liquid flowing into her bowels. Bri had never had an enema before but had read about punishment enemas in erotic novels. She'd always found the descriptions arousing; in fact, the thought of a helpless submissive being filled up with warm, soapy water and then being made to hold it, painfully, until finally being forced to humiliatingly expel it had fueled more than one of her masturbation fantasies.

"It's enough. Too much!" Her pleas fell on deaf ears.

Now she wondered how she could have ever found anything erotic about this sort of punishment. She was in pain and unbearably embarrassed, even if part of her could understand how watching a submissive's private hole cleansed in preparation for her Master's cock might arouse a Dom.

Fuck, fuck, fuck.

She could feel her pussy throbbing and as her juices began to flow, she was furious with herself. Bri shook her head from side to side as she battled between humiliation and the tease of old fantasies from the invasive punishment at the hands of her husband's friends.

Her complaints hadn't worked. She began to

plead with them. "Please... don't do this. I don't know what you want from me!"

James's face was unforgiving as he ignored her begging, monitoring the water flow into her body. With each passing minute, Brianna's cramping was getting worse and the pressure in her bowel more unbearable.

"Too much..." she mumbled and only a few minutes later she cried, "No more! It hurts!"

As her groans of sheer agony got louder and more frequent, James gratefully stopped the flow giving her body a chance to accommodate the liquid before opening the clamp again.

A sheen of sweat soon covered Bri's body, partly from the heat of the warm water filling her, but mostly from the embarrassment and physical strain of trying to retain the liquid in her body. An undeniable sense of surrender was forming in Bri's fragile mind, and with it an odd sort of peace. There was something almost therapeutic in being rendered completely helpless, in being forced to comply with the cleansing her body, as if the flood inside her could wash away her sins when it left her body.

When the huge enema bag was finally empty, James clamped off the tube and immediately began to squeeze a hand pump bulb attached to the hose. Brianna felt the nozzle still shoved up her ass beginning to expand... ballooning to stretch her tightest hole to new and painful limits since she was still sore from Jake's unwanted fucking less than twenty-four hours before. On the one hand, she was grateful for the balloon's presence, which acted as a dam and made it easier to retain the unwanted water. Yet, she was appalled that her ass was being used in a shameful manner yet again.

James finally unhooked the plastic tubing from the balloon plugging her ass and stepped back, wearing a smug expression as he studied her.

The asshole.

"Lukus informed me the more traditional forms of punishment he was using were not having the desired effect. As a basic rule, we discourage orgasms when we're punishing our subs. I'm pretty confident this punishment isn't going to turn into a pleasurable experience for you. Although, I must admit, you may experience euphoria when you're finally allowed to expel, that is, if you can get past the humiliation of expelling in front of Lukus and me."

Brianna decided to press James again. "It's clear you don't think Markus is going to be angry at you for treating me like this, but I wonder what Mary is gonna say when I tell her you're here at the club... touching me... torturing me like this. You're messing with my marriage and I promise you James, I'm going to mess with yours, you asshole."

James gently laughed as he lightly pressed on Bri's distended abdomen, forcing an agonizing groan. "Oh Brianna, you have no idea, do you? Mary is so much more than just my wife. She's my submissive. She has been since we were at Northwestern together with Markus and Lukus. She's been on this very table receiving the exact same punishment when she was naughty, too. I must admit, though... I'm grateful she's managed to remain faithful to me. Lukus would have to hold me back from punishing her until she couldn't walk or sit or move without crying if she ever let someone else's cock touch her. Why do you think Markus isn't here himself? He's a Dom, just like us and he knows he wouldn't be able to control himself when he's this angry. Rule Number One for a Dom is to never punish when you're too angry to control your own emotions. I'm sorry to tell you, but there's no danger of Lukus or me being swayed by your tears or veiled threats."

Her brain was misfiring from the overload of information James had just shared. She was shocked enough to hear that Mary, the woman she'd gone out to dinner with several times, was a submissive. How in the world had she missed all of the signs? She seemed so confident and outgoing as the doting mother of two preteen boys. How the hell did that work, anyway? Clearly there was more to the whole D/s scene that Brianna had no clue about.

But she had trouble believing James's assertion that her husband, the always gentle and loving Markus, was a Dom. Clearly these guys didn't know Markus as well as they thought they did. Before last night, he'd never so much as fucked her hard, let alone displayed any signs of being a dominant Master like Lukus and James clearly were.

She wanted to argue the point, but the pressure to evacuate her bowels was staggering. She closed her eyes in an attempt to calm her ragged breathing and slow her racing heartbeat, and she was completely unprepared when the slap of a wide leather belt hit her tender pussy lips, squarely making contact with her swollen clit and drawing an anguished cry. When she felt the second stroke of the belt make contact with her splayed cunt, her cry turned into an ear-piercing scream.

Her eyes sprung open to watch in disbelief as James pulled his arm back and delivered another full-force belting, this time striking her inner thigh. From her vantage point, Bri could see her creamy skin immediately turn a bright red. The force of the pain crept up on her slowly, turning into an agonizing burn. James continued to rain down his belt, pelting her inner thighs and pussy thoroughly. The only reprieve from the belt came when he leaned over to grab first the left nipple clamp and then the right. As he simultaneously unclamped both tortured tits, the rush of blood through the delicate areas felt like pins and needles poking her nipples.

Brianna was vaguely aware of her own screams. James's torment of her entire body was too much. The barrage of vicious tortures pushed Brianna to that secret destination Lukus had sent her to the night before on stage. As the blows from the belt continued to rain down on her swollen pussy and inner thighs, Brianna allowed her mind to float away.

It was as if she were hovering above the scene now, watching from outside her body. As a captive victim, the pain was nearly unbearable, but as a spectator, the pain was turning into pleasure. The ache of her full lower abdomen had pushed Brianna to the brink of the cliff. The pressure to expel the liquids saturating her body was exquisite, drawing a long, guttural groan.

If the need to expel had her hanging from the edge of the cliff, it was the hard slap of the leather belt that ended up tossing her over, sending her free-falling into a powerful orgasm. Brianna was so far gone in her own pleasurable little world she almost missed her husband's friends' exchange.

"I don't fucking believe it. That was so fast, I didn't even have time to stop and hold her off." James was clearly upset he'd allowed Brianna to orgasm.

Lukus's voice was quiet, almost shaken. "Hell, that was even faster than last night." He nervously ran his hands through his thick, dark hair.

In the wake of her orgasm, Bri's breathing turned shallow and ragged—distressed. She recognized that James had been watching her carefully, and finally took action. Nodding to Lukus, the men each began to release her from the restraints holding her immobile. Once she was free, Lukus scooped her up into his arms like he would a child and rather gently carried her toward the center of the stage.

Embarrassed by her powerful and shameful orgasm, Brianna buried her face into Lukus's neck in a childish attempt to hide, wrapping her arms around his neck. She kept her eyes squeezed tight, trying to focus on not having an accident. She was trying not to think about the fact that Lukus was going to expect her to use the damn bucket as her toilet again.

He stopped mid-stage and effortlessly lifted her body into a sitting position, on a rather tall stool that had wide stirrups similar to the gynecological table. The stirrups were meant to hold her thighs open wide and as she took in the details of the odd chair, she saw there was actually no seat. Her spread upper legs were holding her up, and just below the opening of the seat was a huge bucket.

"Oh my God, no, no, no. Please, Lukus. Don't make me do this. I'm begging you." She reached out, desperately grabbing his tee-shirt, trying to pull him to her. She was shaking her head in disbelief. Not here. Even with the club empty, they couldn't expect her to do this here, in front of them both, splayed open and on display. Her tears were flowing again. She made a feeble attempt to lift herself off the stirrups, but Lukus easily held her in place.

His answer came in the form of a whisper against her ear. "Don't make me get the rope to tie you down, Bri. You know you need to do this. I promise—you'll feel better when you're done." All traces of anger seemed to have dissipated. What remained was concern.

As her ragged breaths became increasingly labored, James reached beneath her to deflate the balloon in her ass. He was nice enough to give her a warning before he started to remove it. "Okay, it's coming out now Brianna."

Brianna was physically shaking from the strain on her body, the fear of the loss of control over her most private bodily functions, and the cool air hitting her sweat-covered skin. She was squeezing her eyes closed tightly in an attempt to forget where she was long enough to allow her body to relax enough to expel. And even though she'd decided to comply and release the enema, she found her body just wouldn't cooperate.

Several agonizing minutes ticked by. When her shaking approached actual convulsions, she vaguely heard Lukus say, "Fuck this." He scooped her up into his arms, clutching her tightly against his warm chest. Brianna wrapped her arms around his neck and buried her face against him as she let the sobs consume her. She was crying so hard she barely caught Lukus's words.

"Go home, James. I'm sorry I dragged you down here today. I'll talk to you later."

CHAPTER FOURTEEN

LUKUS

Lukus pushed through the door at the back of the stage, rushing through the backstage dungeon, through his office, and into the small elevator that barely fit them both. He struggled to lean down to push the button that would take them up to his loft. He prayed Brianna could hold it a bit longer or he would find himself with a major mess on his hands.

It would serve you right if she can't hold it, you asshole.

The guilt he'd been pushing down since last night was back with a vengeance. Brianna was not an informed member of the club and she hadn't had a clue what she'd signed up for. No matter what she'd done, she didn't deserve this kind of humiliation. Markus was just gonna have to get his divorce the old-fashioned way—through the courts.

He's a lawyer, for Christ's sake. He shouldn't need me to do his dirty work for him.

Lukus was relieved her convulsing had slowed to mere shivering by the time the elevator doors opened. He rushed through the great room in his loft, through his huge master bedroom, relieved when he finally arrived at the door to his luxurious master bathroom. He lowered Brianna's feet to the floor, making sure she was steady before releasing her. Her eyes were closed tightly, trying to shut out what was happening to her.

"Brianna, open your eyes, sweetheart. Look at me." All traces of his anger with her were gone and when she opened her eyes, he hoped she could see he was being sincere.

Lukus reached out to stroke a lone tear away from her cheek with the pad of his thumb. "I never should have pushed you like this. I'm sorry. I blackmailed you into putting your signature on the club papers and I know you had no idea what you were signing up for. I'm gonna leave you alone for a while. If you need me, just call out, okay?"

With her panic receding, Brianna looked weary. All evidence of her earlier strength and bravado, gone. She nodded, but as he turned to leave, she called out to him. "Lukus?" Her voice was barely a whisper. "Thank you."

"You're welcome, Brianna." He watched as she turned and closed the door behind her.

Lukus wasted no time beelining it to his well-stocked wet bar. He didn't give a shit that it wasn't even noon; nothing was going to stop him from pouring himself a tall whiskey. He downed the king-sized shot in one gulp, letting it burn his throat on the way to his churning stomach. He poured a second before walking away from the bar and turning toward the window.

It was this view of the Chicago skyline that had been the selling point when he bought the empty building over six years ago. He'd been looking for a space to open his club but hadn't expected to find a place to live at the same time. He'd known he was home the first time he experienced the unfettered view from the top floor of the seven-story building. He'd spent a full year converting the first three floors into The Punishment Pit, complete with a half dozen guest apartments. The top—a high-ceilinged loft—had morphed into his private sanctuary with a small private theater, half basketball court, and full weight room.

The following year, he managed to remodel the middle floors into the new home for his already thriving security business. He'd installed a street-side entrance on the opposite side of the building from the club's alley entrance. He'd worried it would be difficult to mesh the divergent parts of his life so closely, but he'd worried for nothing. The only downside now was that managing everything under one roof gave him little reason to leave the building.

Lukus found himself in a rare mood this morning,

no doubt the direct result of being brought to his knees by the feelings caused by Brianna's presence. The guilt he understood. It made sense to him. It was the deeper emotions that he had yet to come to terms with.

He'd left her in the bathroom, and he hoped she'd stay in there until he got his head on straight.

Lukus was a man of action, so spending time analyzing feelings was not how he'd normally choose to spend a Saturday morning. There was no other choice today. He couldn't turn off his brain—or other body parts, for that matter—not even if he wanted to. He was enough of a realist to know he needed to face the situation, and he didn't like where that led him.

I'm jealous, completely and insanely jealous, of Markus. Fuck me.

Like a bullet between the eyes, it hit him that Brianna was the first woman he'd met that came even close to that elusive balance of strength and submission he'd been seeking for years. In many ways, she reminded him of Mary, only she was a hundred times better. No offense to Mary, but Lukus had never once been tempted to cross the line with James's wife in spite of frequently disciplining her in very intimate ways. While she was the right balance of strength and submission, she was never his type physically, not to mention she only had eyes for her husband.

But Brianna... hell, she was the real deal. She was the kind of woman who was the picture-perfect wife on your arm at an important business dinner and the slutty whore in your bedroom when you got home. He'd watched her struggling with her deep submissive tendencies, but she never once had let him push her to a point where she forgot who she was at her core. The defiance in her eyes as she stood up to him—the resolve that made her fight for her crumbling marriage—it made him want to turn her over his knee for a good, hard, intimate spanking and then immediately pull her into his protective arms to gently wipe away her tears and make sweet love to her.

I'm so fucked. I don't do 'gentle,' 'sweet,' or 'love.'

He understood why Markus was completely broken at the thought of losing her. Lukus felt the same sense of loss at the idea of her leaving, and she wasn't even his to lose. Her big, expressive, chocolate-brown eyes. That beautiful, tight, tanned body. Hell, he usually preferred blondes, but he even loved the feel of her long, dark hair running through his fingers. He could imagine holding it in a tight ponytail, using it to pull her body back onto his cock while he fucked her hard from behind. She was so responsive he could just hear her begging him to fuck her harder. Her body was made to enjoy the delicate balance of pain and pleasure he'd spent much of his adult life learning to deliver.

Turning away from the windows, Lukus sank into the nearby lounge chair. Kicking his feet up on the ottoman, he took a long drag from his whiskey, steeling himself. It took longer than normal, but he managed to rein in his emotions.

Logically, he knew Brianna was a dead end for him. He'd already failed his friend, and the sooner he could get her out of this building and back with her husband, the better off they'd all be. He may have been a ruthless bastard, but even he knew better than to fuck his friend's wife unless they had some sort of prior arrangement. Lukus knew Markus would never want to share his wife with anyone, not even his best friend. Not after everything that had happened. That put her off limits. Period.

So now what?

His first thought was to bundle her up and drive her ass home to her husband the very second she walked out of his bathroom. He could ring the doorbell and leave her on the front porch like an unwanted puppy for Markus to find and deal with.

But Lukus knew he couldn't do that. Not to Brianna and not to his friend. Lukus may have never been married, but he knew a little something about the delicate balance of successful D/s relationships and if one thing was clear to Lukus, Markus and Brianna were in desperate need of help navigating through the secrets they'd obviously been keeping from each other. Markus may have thought he wanted a divorce, but it was just his wounded pride talking. He was the stupidest man on the face of earth if he didn't wake up and fight to save his marriage with Brianna.

Finally feeling like he had a way forward, Lukus stood and headed to the kitchen where he poured the rest of the whiskey down the drain. He was gonna need his wits about him today if he was going to navigate safely through the emotional minefield he was about to enter. He may not be following Markus's instructions, but if he did his job right, Markus was going to end up owing Lukus a hell of a lot more than Lukus ever owed him.

Tiffany

"Hey, you feeling okay? You don't look well." Kennedy brushed Tiffany's forearm lightly to get her attention.

Doing her best to put on a happy face, Tiffany smiled before replying. "Oh sure, I'm just really tired today."

Her friend smiled indulgently, "So you still haven't been able to get ahold of her, eh?"

Tiff should have known better than to hide the truth of what was bothering her from Kennedy. Still, she wasn't going to go into the gory details of exactly what she was really worried about. How could she?

It's not every day you're worried that your best

friend is either kidnapped, raped, or dead—or worse, all of the above.

"Bri and Markus were going out to dinner last night. I'm sure she's just home, in bed, nursing the mother of all hangovers."

Even as she said the words, Tiffany prayed they were true. When Bri had been ten, twenty, even thirty minutes late, that explanation had sufficed. Now that she was three *hours* late, that excuse was out the window. Bri was often tardy, but she always answered her cell phone. And not once had she ever been a no-call/no-show to work. It had been a real pain in the ass to juggle Bri's appointments around, especially since Tiff didn't know if she'd be coming in at all or not.

On a normal day, she might pass it off that Bri's phone had run out of battery or some other benign reason for her best friend going dark on her. But today was anything but normal. Knowing that Jake was in Chicago, that Brianna had planned to talk to her husband about her submissive sexual needs the night before, and add that both Markus and Brianna were incommunicado—that meant nothing today was routine.

Tiffany used a lull between appointments to hide out in the salon office to make more calls. After Bri's phone went straight to voicemail again, she switched over and tried to call Markus for the third time. While his phone at least rang several times, it too eventually rolled to voicemail. Finally desperate, she left a message.

"Hey, Markus... It's Tiff." She paused, stumbling through what to say since she had absolutely no idea what Bri had or had not discussed with her husband. "I'm worried about Brianna." Unwilling to outright say she didn't know where Bri was, she finally added. "Call me. Please."

Tiff pressed END before switching over to her contact list. She'd already called Brianna's brother to try to inconspicuously ask if he'd heard from her. She flirted with another idea, but she didn't really want to call Bri's mom. Not only would that call turn into a talkfest, but alerting Bri's mom that there might be a problem would be like calling in an airstrike to neutralize a bug. It might get the job done, but the extended fallout wouldn't be worth it.

She didn't know what to make of both Markus and Brianna going dark on her at the same time. Her mind raced with worst case scenarios. Had they been in a car accident? As bad as that sounded, thinking of Markus losing it after finding out Brianna had gone anywhere with Jake the day before made Tiffany even more upset.

Why did I push her so hard to come clean? What if Markus won't forgive her? It'll be all my fault.

Tiff had been furious with Bri for not only falling for Jake's bullshit again the day before, but also for putting Tiff into the position to lie to Markus. But now that Bri was missing, all anger was gone, replaced with a growing dread.

Something is really wrong.

Tiffany looked at her Apple Watch for the hundredth time. Oddly, time was dragging and flying simultaneously. She didn't know for sure what was going on, but she made up her mind to take action. She had a nail appointment arriving in a few minutes, but if she hadn't heard from Bri or Markus by the time it was over, she'd have Kennedy fill in so she could get in the car and drive over to the Lamberts. If they weren't there, she'd have no choice but to call the asshole, Jake.

One way or another, she would find out what the hell was going on.

CHAPTER FIFTEEN

BRIANNA

Brianna's relief was overwhelming, both physically and emotionally. James had been right about experiencing an almost euphoric high as she finally purged the overflowing liquids from her body in a rush. It wasn't exactly orgasmic, but it certainly had stirred dark, submissive desires within her. Her feeling of complete surrender had turned into a form of joy at the prospect of being symbolically cleansed of her sins from the inside out.

Now that the initial wave of relief had passed, Bri had the time to contemplate the gravity of what had happened to her since Lukus had taken her out of the cage. The complex emotions raging through her were beyond confusing. Her body's deep desire to submit was at war with the part of her brain that wanted to reason her way out of the situation.

Lukus and James had been harsh, and yet on some level she accepted that she deserved what they'd put her through. So why had Lukus finally caved in and rescued her from the humiliation of having to expel out in the open in front of her husband's friends?

Who cares why he did it, Bri? Just thank God he did.

Still, Brianna couldn't stop herself from analyzing Lukus's motives. From what little she knew of him, she suspected she'd glimpsed a side of Lukus few others had seen—a vulnerable side he worked hard to hide from the world.

She was also surprised at herself. As horrible as she felt for letting Jake con her into leaving with him the day before instead of calling the police like Tiffany had begged, Bri was more sure than ever that she needed to fight until her last breath to make it up to Markus. As afraid as she was about what other humiliating punishments Lukus had planned, she was even more terrified Markus wouldn't give her a chance at forgiveness. She needed to stay strong and stop letting her own fear press her into tears.

Lukus was every bit as sadistic as Jake had ever been, but in spite of all of the horrendous things he'd done to her in the last twelve hours, he still seemed somehow trustworthy. She'd seen him watching her carefully while James was punishing her. It was as if he were standing guard, making sure she wasn't truly hurt. Remembering his protectiveness made her heart flutter.

Could it be true that Markus had been a member

LIVIA GRANT

of the Punishment Pit before meeting her? On the surface, she'd have said it was impossible, and yet she saw many similarities between the two strong men. Bri had absolutely no trouble believing they were best friends. Hell, they even looked alike. On a professional level, Markus was as alpha male as Lukus any day. It was only in private they were so different. So why in the world had Markus completely hidden his dominant nature from her?

If only he'd been honest with me from the start, we might have been able to avoid this whole mess in the first place.

That pesky voice in her head cried bullshit on herself, reminding her she'd been silent about her own taboo sexual needs as well.

Bri spent over twenty minutes alone in Lukus's private bathroom before she finally felt ready to face him again. When she opened the bathroom door, Lukus was waiting just a few inches away, leaning casually against the door jamb. He had a tall glass of ice water in his hand, holding it out for her. "Here. Drink this. You haven't had enough liquids."

The water was like heaven and she drank it all.

Handing the glass back to her unlikely host, Brianna felt a small sense of relief. She still had no clue how she was going to convince her husband to forgive her, but she knew she couldn't give up trying yet.

"So now what?" she asked quietly.

"Now, I take you back into the bathroom and run

you a hot bath. Then we're going to talk and you're gonna explain to me why the hell you cheated on Markus. It's abundantly clear to me that you do love him and I have my suspicions... but I need to hear it from you."

"Why do you care?" she asked. "Why not let me call Tiffany and have her pick me up? You could just get rid of me."

"As tempting as that sounds, I really do owe Markus. He pulled my ass out of the fire this week so I'm not just going to shirk my responsibilities. He entrusted you to me, so you're stuck with me." For the briefest of moments, Lukus's face softened before his dominant mask returned. "Don't think just because I've backed off all of a sudden that I'm any less pissed that you hurt my best friend. I was there. I saw his face when you broke his heart. You still have a lot of explaining to do and, mark my words, if I don't like the answers, your punishment will continue indefinitely until you sign the fucking divorce papers. Understand, sweetheart?"

Brianna broke into her first smile since meeting him. "You talk big, but you really are a pretty nice guy, you know that, Lukus?"

Lukus snorted and was about to answer, but Bri cut him off, holding up her hand to silence him.

"Don't worry. Your secret's safe with me. I promise not to let anyone know the Master has a heart."

He shook his head, looking uncomfortable with

her teasing. Recovering, Lukus grabbed her by the elbow to tow her back into the bathroom. "Come along, little girl. Time is wasting."

Lukus marched her to the sink and rooted around in the cabinet below, coming out with a brand-new toothbrush. Next, he dug in a drawer for toothpaste, leaving her behind to brush her teeth while he headed to an enormous whirlpool tub in his luxurious master bath.

She kept tabs on him in the reflection of the huge mirror. The tub was on a raised platform and Lukus knelt on the marble steps, leaning in to start the water. He reached into the nearby cabinet for what looked like feminine bath oils. It was then that Bri wondered just how many other women had enjoyed a bath in Lukus's private haven.

Brianna had joined him next to the bath by the time the tub was full. A lilac scent wafted up from the warm steam. Lukus turned on the whirlpool jets before reaching back to assist Brianna. She self-consciously allowed the robe she'd donned before opening the door for him to drop as she climbed the steps and lowered into the luxurious bath.

A groan of unadulterated bliss escaped Brianna's lips as the heated water began to soothe her sore and weary body. She sunk back, closing her eyes, and lay her head against the soft bath pillow conveniently waiting for her tired head. She lost track of time as she enjoyed the feel of water from the powerful jets pulsing against her aching muscles.

She snapped back with a jolt, surprised to see Lukus still sitting on the side of the tub, his eyes watching her intently, an unreadable expression on his face.

"I'm so sorry. It felt so good, I kind of lost it for a few minutes," she stammered. Suddenly self-conscious, she lifted her knees enough to try to hide her pussy while raising her hands to cover her exposed breasts. "Are you gonna sit there and watch me? It's kind of creeping me out."

Lukus's face broke out into a broad smile. "Really? After all we've experienced together in the last twenty-four hours, it's having me watch you bathe that has you creeped out?"

Bri chuckled. "Well when you put it that way, it does sound ridiculous. But still, I really can take a bath by myself, you know."

"I know. But it's been my experience that women open up better in the comfort of a whirlpool tub. Of course, I usually like to climb in with them and, well, encourage them, if you know what I mean. Unfortunately, that doesn't seem to be the smartest of ideas today so I thought you could start answering some of my questions while I soap your back and wash your hair."

Bri's heart fluttered at the thought of Lukus helping her bathe. While it was true he'd inspected her most hidden body parts, having him wash her back and hair ridiculously seemed more intimate. She felt like she should say no, but when he grabbed a bath sponge and lathered it up with body soap, the objection died in her throat. She told herself he was still the Master, and she was just following orders as she'd agreed to do. But deep down, she feared they were both feeling the same dangerous tug of something she was afraid to acknowledge.

"So, why don't you start at the beginning," Lukus urged. "Who the fuck is Jake and why the hell did you feel the need for the touching reunion?"

"Seriously. We're really going to have this very personal discussion here... now... while I'm naked in the tub?"

"You bet. Like I said, I suspect you won't be able to hide the truth from me here."

"Honestly, Lukus. I don't want to hide anything. Not anymore."

"If it makes you feel any better, Markus has done his share of hiding secrets too. For two people who love each other so much, you both seem to be very good at lying to each other." His tone was hard.

"I don't feel like I lied to Markus," she snapped, before softening. "At least, not in the beginning. Only later, after I'd healed did I start having to hide my feelings from him."

"Healed? What the hell does that mean? Were you sick?"

Bri feared discussing her private sexual experiences with Lukus, but she pushed it down. He was, after all, the Master of a private sex club. If he couldn't understand what she'd been through, she had no chance of helping Markus understand. Brianna closed her eyes and started her story as the jets of water continued to relax her body.

"Not sick in the way you think." She took a deep breath and began. "I knew by the time I was starting college that there was something wrong with me. Most of my friends were pairing up with nice boys who were complete pushovers. And they were happy with these guys. After all, it's the twenty-first century. Why should men call all the shots? But all I saw when I looked at these guys were total wimps. Of course, my friends all kept trying to set me up with guys like they had and so I'd date perfectly nice, normal guys to make them happy. But the more I dated *normal* guys, the more frustrated I got.

"Do you know how exasperating it is to verbalize your submissive needs to a guy too clueless to figure it out and too weak to fulfill those needs even if he knew? It kind of defeats the purpose to have to spell it out... not that it mattered. Just the mention of the word 'spanking' had the ones I did tell bolting faster than a racecar driver at Daytona."

"Bri, look at me." His sternly issued interruption startled her into instant obedience. "Sweetheart, there's nothing wrong with you or these feelings you have. You know that, right?" He didn't give her a chance to answer. "I don't ever want to hear you say there's something wrong with you again." He nodded. "Go on."

Bri settled back against the tub and continued. "I

guess an important part of the story is that in high school I loved romance novels, but over time I realized the normal-boy-meets-normal-girl-happily-ever-after stories just weren't cutting it for me. I gravitated to the edgy romances where the woman was always the submissive to a dominant, strong man. You know—the naughty princess is captured by the rogue pirate and ravaged at sea until he admits he loves her, and they live happily ever after. Or the naughty young socialite who marries the older Duke who spanks her into becoming a well-behaved young wife while loving and cherishing her till death do they part. Over time, I found a lot of spanking and domestic discipline sites on the Internet and that led to more aggressive BDSM sites and before long... I knew I wasn't gonna be happy unless I was with a dominant man who would not only love me, but protect me, discipline me, and basically want to master me—at least in the bedroom.

"For years I kept those desires pushed down. Then in college I met my best friend Tiffany. She not only understood but shared many of my same... well... hang-ups." Bri opened her eyes to look into Lukus's for the rest of the story. "I know we were stupid, but after college, Tiff and I started hanging out at some of the BDSM clubs downtown. We were smart enough to always stick together and at first; we just went to watch. I was still too timid to actually cross over from a voyeur to a player and honestly, I was happy enough keeping it that way for a long time. But then I met Jake. He was my first and I guess my only BDSM relationship."

"How old were you when you met him?"

"Twenty-two. A baby really."

"So, what happened?"

"The first few months or so things were okay. I can't say I was truly happy. Not in the way I am with Markus, but I was certainly having fun exploring all of the darker sexual experiences I'd been reading and fantasizing about. And Jake was happy helping me explore them. Eventually, though, things started to change. I'd pretty much plateaued and was happy with the spanking and having sex a little on the rough side. Jake, on the other hand, had decided he wanted to keep pushing the envelope."

"It truly is one of the hardest parts in a D/s relationship," Lukus said. "The figuring out each other's limits and understanding if the Dom and sub are compatible."

"Well, that assumes that both people actually *want* to discover each other's limits."

Lukus's face hardened. "He was a new Dom. I gather he didn't take it slow enough for you. I try so hard to take new Doms under my wing to help them out. So many assholes think that being a Dom means you just get to be a domineering jerk twenty-four-seven. They don't realize the great responsibility that comes with taking care of a submissive. Subs are to be protected... nurtured... cherished."

"Well, Jake must have missed getting that memo,"

LIVIA GRANT

Brianna said with a mirthless laugh. "He had no interest in understanding my limits. On the contrary, he wasn't happy unless he was pushing me well past them." Bri took a break, hating to say the next words, but knowing she couldn't stop. "I should have left the first time he raped me, but the lines between submission and abuse were so fuzzy for me at first. He said all of the right words to keep me confused. *'You told me you like to submit, so you'll submit.'* Or my all-time favorite—*'subs have no right to say no... ever.'*"

"The fucker. I thought I was pissed at him yesterday. Today, I think I'm gonna kill him. Did Markus know about him?"

"Yeah, he knew. By the time I finally left Jake, he'd pretty much beaten me within an inch of my life more than once—all in the name of punishment, mind you. I think the worst thing I ever did to deserve a punishment was forget to pick up his dry cleaning before one of his business trips. I left him for a couple months after that session. But then he came around with a big bouquet of roses, begging for another chance just before Valentine's Day. He was always so apologetic, swearing he'd learned his lesson and that he'd never let his anger get the most of him ever again. That time he booked us a weekend away at a bed and breakfast to prove he could be as romantic as the next guy. Like a fool, I went away with him."

Bri stopped the story there. Her eyes were closed again as she started to tremble.

Lukus cleared his throat. "Is the water getting too cold? You're shivering."

Her eyes remained closed, trying to shut out her memories as she shook her head. "The water is fine. I was just deciding how much I was going to tell you. I made the mistake of telling Markus everything and I think it's a big part of what went wrong between us."

"Sweetheart, you need to tell me what you told Markus. I need to know where his head is at right now."

Brianna turned to gaze into the eyes of her husband's best friend. "Why do you call me sweetheart?"

Her question seemed to catch Lukus off-guard. "I don't know. I guess at first I was using it to get your attention. Now... it sort of just fits. Does it bother you?"

"It should... but oddly it doesn't." She gave him a pained smile. "It's just that Markus calls me sweetheart, too."

Their eyes were locked. The energy in the room was shifting but Lukus broke the connection first, looking away. "I think you're stalling." Reaching into the water, Lukus lifted her left leg and began to lather her with the soapy bath sponge. "Back to your story."

Brianna looked away from him, her mind wandering back to the weekend that would forever change her life. "I should have known when we arrived at the remote cabin in the woods that something was wrong. Jake made out that he just wanted us to have a romantic getaway all alone. But what he really wanted was to get me miles away from civilization so no one could hear me screaming. We weren't in the cabin ten minutes before he had me stripped naked and tied down. There was nothing romantic about it. The sole purpose of the weekend was for him to beat me until I promised never to leave him again. I've blocked out a lot of the details. I only remember that he used every punishment implement he owned on me. He only took breaks from beating me to get something to eat or rape me. Before we left on the trip, he'd promised me he would finally let me have a safeword, but of course the first time I tried to use it, he laughed and said no one knew my limits better than he did and that he'd only stop when he thought I'd had enough."

Brianna turned her face back to Lukus. Tears she'd been holding back were now spilling down her face.

"Funny thing is that he never thought I'd had enough. By the time he dropped me off at home on Sunday night, my entire body was one huge bruise. I had over two dozen open cuts or wounds. I had rope burns, bruised ribs, and it took over a month for my..." Bri dropped her eyes and took a ragged breath before continuing. "I was so torn from the rough sex that it took months to recover. Tiffany begged me to call the police or at least go to the hospital. Looking back, of course I should have, but I was in shock. It was the only time I ever got fired from a job, but I just couldn't bring myself to leave our apartment for weeks."

Lukus's face contorted with rage. He threw the sponge he'd been holding against the wall and clenched his fist.

"Lukus, please calm down. The look on your face reminds me of the day I told Markus. He was ready to kill Jake, too."

It was clear that Lukus was on the verge of losing control, but Brianna was completely unprepared when he reached out and roughly grabbed her arms, jerking her forward until there was little space between them. Despite how close they were, he was screaming at her. "Are you shitting me? It's not Jake I'm ready to kill right now. What the hell were you thinking, going anywhere with him ever again? The bastard should be in jail. It's bad enough that he hurt you in the past, but Jesus fucking Christ, Brianna! How stupid are you that you actually let him near you ever again? He could have really hurt you... or even worse. No wonder Markus is crushed. You didn't just cheat on him. You cheated on him with a sadistic fucking rapist! How do you think that makes Markus feel? You might as well have castrated him! It couldn't have hurt him any worse."

His words hit home. Brianna was shattered. She'd been so selfishly worried about her own predicament she'd truly never stopped to look at this through Markus's eyes. He'd given up his dominant side just to prove to Brianna that he was nothing like the man who had abused her. That she would cheat on him with that very man was the ultimate betrayal.

No wonder he wants a divorce. He must hate me.

Her tears were back as Lukus continued to stare her down with his rage-filled green eyes. "Don't you dare even try to use your tears on me again, Brianna. I'm so fucking angry with you right now that it's taking every ounce of my self-control to stop from dragging your ass out of this tub and paddling you until you can't sit down for a week. The only thing stopping me is I refuse to do anything close to what that prick Jake would do in this situation. It makes me sick that I might ever be put into the same category as an asshole like him."

"I'm so sorry, Lukus. Truly, I know how stupid I was. Even though he has shit that he's blackmailing me with, I've messed this up so badly."

Doubt wrinkled his forehead. "You mentioned that last night on stage, but I didn't believe you. What kind of blackmail could he possibly have that would make you betray Markus?" Lukus questioned.

"It's complicated. It's mostly bogus shit from our past that not only implicates me, but Tiffany... her brothers. Shit, I should have listened to Tiffany."

Bri trailed off, but Lukus pressed her. "Yes, you should have, but I need more information. What does he have? Pictures?"

"Yes, and... worse."

"What's worse? Video?" He was guessing.

"All of the above. I totally screwed up six months ago, and let him convince me to meet him—and, shit, we had sex— but I hated myself the moment it as over. I swore I'd never talk to him again—but I didn't know he took pictures. I only went with him yesterday because he promised to give me a hard drive with all of the pictures. I told him I'd only stay in public areas, but... like always... he tricked me. I should have known better." That's when it hit Brianna. "I have no idea how much you and Markus heard yesterday when you were listening in, but you have to know, I wasn't in that room willingly. He was just supposed to give me the hard drive. But once I was behind closed doors, he put tape over my mouth to keep me from screaming. He tied me down. He..."

Brianna let her voice trail off. *Did it really make any difference?*

"He what?" There was tension in Lukus's voice and his jaw looked locked as he waited for her to say the words she didn't want to say.

Their eyes met. "Does it still count as rape if he made me come?"

Lukus sucked in a deep breath, exhaling slowly. They sat in silence long enough she wasn't sure he would answer her. When he did, she didn't like what he had to say. "It didn't sound like rape."

"Didn't you hear me warning him I'd call 911? Screaming for help before he gagged me?"

"Sorry, sweetheart. All we heard was him belting you and you clearly loving it. We heard him talking about taking your ass and making fun of Markus, calling him Vanilla, and promising to come see you the next time he was in town. And of course, we heard you coming over and over."

"Dammit! If you were gonna listen in, you should have listened to everything." She felt desperation closing in. "I just wanted the hard drive. He promised he'd give it to me. I was frantic to get the evidence so both Tiffany and I could finally relax. Shit, she begged me not to go, to call the police instead. She's angry with me, too, just like you are. Like Markus. Oh, God. He really is going to divorce me, isn't he? I'm going to lose Markus and Tiffany both."

Brianna had been trying so hard to stay strong but hearing that Markus had only heard the damning parts of her time with Jake only made things worse. She finally succumbed, letting her sobs consume her as the guilt from her betrayal of the two most important people in her life threatened to drown her.

I have no one to blame but myself. I had it all and I threw it all away. Please, God, let them forgive me.

CHAPTER SIXTEEN

LUKUS

Lukus was torn as he watched Brianna melt down before his eyes. Part of him wanted to kill her himself for being so stupid. The other part wanted to hold her and tell her everything was going to be okay.

I'm so fucked.

As she cried inconsolably, he knew he needed to take control, but he wasn't sure if he could cross those lines again. If he'd known what had really happened with Jake the day before he never would have put her on stage or punished her the way he had. He could only hope he hadn't added to the trauma that asshole had put her through... but it was also becoming clear that Markus's avoidance of anything BDSM was the core issue between them. It was time Brianna started to understand what being a submissive was really about.

"That's it," he said. "I'm doing you no favors by

letting you get away with this. Stop crying... right now."

Lukus roughly pulled Bri closer, completely oblivious to the water drenching him and sloshing to the floor. His grip was tight on her upper arms and he kept his gaze hard, yet he managed to wait patiently for her to calm down enough to listen. It took Bri several moments to catch her breath.

When she was finally still, he spoke. "You're gonna listen to me, and more importantly, you're going to believe every word I say. Do you hear me, little girl?" When she didn't answer, he grabbed her long hair and yanked her closer, their faces only inches apart. "Answer me. Are you listening?"

"Yes." It was barely a whisper.

"First, you have never, and I mean this—*never*—been in a BDSM relationship. You were in an abusive relationship. That asshole was not a Dom. He was a criminal, a bully who took advantage of your extraordinarily high tolerance for pain to terrorize you for his own enjoyment." His eyes bore into hers, trying to burn his words into her brain—he needed to know she'd gotten the message. "Tell me you understand what I just told you, Bri."

When she stared at him blankly, he gently shook her and when that failed, he pulled her over the edge of the tub, exposing her wet ass. Lukus wasted no time in swatting her butt with his open hand a dozen times. When he pulled her back to his arms, he saw the fire flashing in her eyes and knew he had her full attention.

"Let's try this again, sweetheart. Have you ever been in a D/s relationship?"

"It's just words, Lukus... a label. What difference does it make?"

He answered her by roughly returning her to the edge of the tub to deliver another dozen swats. This time when he pulled her up close, he saw fresh tears in her eyes.

Shit, I want to hold her so bad it hurts.

"Are you listening now?"

"Yes, you asshole! Stop spanking me." She tried swatting at his drenched shirt.

Damn her.

It'd been so long since he'd had a woman with her spirit giving him shit back... and even longer since he *liked* it. Lukus couldn't hide his amused smile before continuing on. "I'll stop when I know you're listening. I've been a Dom my entire adult life. I've made a career out of disciplining submissives. I've certainly made most of them cry and even sometimes scream, but never... and I do mean never, have I truly hurt anyone. Everyone had a safeword and everyone wanted it, *needed* it. They knew exactly what they were signing up for before..."

His words trailed off as a crush of his own guilt arrived, realizing he could no longer make that assertion ever again. Not after what he'd done the night before in the name of friendship. The guilt must have been plastered all over his face because Brianna's knowing eyes mocked him.

"Everyone except me. That's why you stopped today, isn't it?" she asked quietly.

Lukus didn't even try to hide his remorse. "Yes, and I'm sorry. It would kill me if you ever lumped me in with assholes like Jake. If you thought I could hurt you like he did..." He suddenly felt so defenseless, like a little boy looking for absolution.

To his relief, Brianna's lips curved up slightly. "I can't explain it, but in spite of all of the things you've done to me, I know I'm safe with you, Lukus. I've been afraid, of course, but I saw you watching me today as if you were taking care of me. I never... not one single minute... felt like Jake was taking care of me."

"I wish..." He let the words die away.

Shut the fuck up, dipshit. You're about to cross the line.

Brianna picked up his sentence, saving him from making a mistake. "I wish I knew what I could do to make this up to Markus. Oh God, Lukus... he's never going to forgive me. He's going to divorce me." Her panic had returned with the memory of her husband's anger.

The Dom had left the building. Lukus's own guilt left him vulnerable, an emotion he hadn't felt in... well, almost never. The unique woman before him was stripping him bare. It was as if she were a drug to him and as hard as he tried to resist, the craving to hold her was all consuming.

Lukus didn't stop Bri when she closed the last inches between them to lay her head on his chest, letting her broken-hearted sobs wrack her. At first, he restrained himself from comforting her, but when she started to hyperventilate, he reached into the water to lift her wet, soapy body against his already drenched shirt.

"Let's get you dried off," he said, helping her to stand before reaching for a fluffy towel.

Brianna allowed him to towel her off, not even resisting as he lifted her to carry her to the bedroom. When he laid her down, he waited for her crying to subside. But it only got worse as she imagined the worst case about her marriage.

He knew it was a mistake even as he was doing it, yet he couldn't stop himself. He wanted to hold her. Removing his wet t-shirt, he lay down beside her, coaxing Brianna from her balled-up position as he took her into his arms. She rested her head against his chest, wrapping her left arm and leg across his body. She was holding onto him for dear life, and he held her in return, gently stroking her damp hair, caressing her back, her arms... comforting her with soft whispers as she broke down.

"Shhh. It's gonna be okay." He waited for her to cry it out, knowing that as soon as her meltdown ended, things were going to get more complicated. He'd long ago blown past his ethical line, yet he couldn't bring himself to let her go. Brianna's body was curled up against him, seeking his comfort, his protection. It was too damn much and yet it wasn't even close to enough.

Never before had the desire to have it all slammed him so hard. Lukus wanted this woman so badly his heart actually ached. He wanted to consume her, own her, punish her for being stupid, kiss her until she was happy again, and then fuck her until she screamed with pleasure. Yet, he knew he couldn't have those things and still look himself in the mirror.

She belongs to Markus.

Brianna made the first move to pull away, no doubt sensing the dangerous line they were flirting with crossing. Lukus held her tight until she started to wiggle free, finally lifting her head to look into his eyes. He recognized the almost feral look of desire in her brown orbs. He knew he was mirroring the same desire in return. Time stood still—his breath hitched, neither of them moving.

Lukus turned his brain off and let instinct take over. He rolled over, trapping Brianna's lithe body beneath him. He placed his elbows on either side of her damp head—their faces so close they could feel each other's breath. He ran her thick hair through his fingers. The feel of her bare breasts under his hard chest was like an electric current welding them together. She had to feel his erection pressing into her, gently grinding as if he were thrusting into her.

Only his jeans protected them from the madness of proceeding.

The power she held over him was intoxicating. He saw the desire in her eyes, desire for him, desire for his domination. It was a toss-up whose breath was more labored, whose heart was racing the fastest.

I have to taste her. Just one taste.

Lukus moved in slow motion, subconsciously giving her time to stop him. He first lowered his forehead to hers, making yet another intimate connection as he began to close the final few inches that separated their lips, stopping just a fraction before they physically touched. He could smell the minty toothpaste she had used just minutes before. His vulnerability was back. He knew he shouldn't just take what he wanted. Not from Brianna.

Still, he moved to close the final inch, desperate to claim her mouth in a heated kiss. At the final second, Brianna turned her head, forcing him to move his empty lips to the crook of her neck. He sucked her tender skin, overcome with the desire to mark her as his own. He felt heady when Bri shuddered from the pleasure rippling through her as he sucked and nibbled.

Only her crying out his name finally brought him to his senses. "Lukus! Please... stop. We can't do this. Not to Markus. I'm begging you. Please... stop."

With great effort, Lukus rolled away from her, landing on his back. His breath was still labored as he threw his forearm over his eyes, too ashamed of himself to even look at her.

Thank God she was strong enough to stop us.

They lay silently for several minutes, each lost in thought. Lukus was the first to speak. "Say I believe you that you didn't go there to cheat on Markus yesterday. You still need to make me understand why the hell you'd go anywhere with Jake six months ago."

"Seriously? That's what you want to talk about right now? After..." Bri's voice wavered.

"There's nothing to talk about. You belong to Markus. I was stupid. It won't happen again. Now tell me."

He didn't dare look at her yet. He was grateful that she answered his question.

"After the cabin, I was so fucked up that I needed to learn to trust men all over again. I told Markus about Jake right after we started dating. There was no way I could hide it. I was afraid he'd see me as damaged goods, but he was so understanding. He was exactly what I needed at the time. So sweet. So gentle. So loving. He helped me recover and truly, I love everything about him. He is wonderful to me. It's just..." She stopped and sighed.

Lukus finished her thought for her, the answer obvious. "It's just that after you recovered, you started to miss the edginess and excitement of turning over control. After watching you respond to punishments and knowing you can hit subspace faster than anyone else I've ever been with, I can only imagine how much you missed being dominated. That was the one thing that Markus wasn't giving you." Lukus paused, putting more of the puzzle pieces together before adding, "It's starting to make sense now. I never understood how Markus could just walk away from the lifestyle. He's a charter member of the club. He and Georgie came here often. Then the next thing I know he divorces Georgie, meets you, and decides to go all Mr. Rogers on me. He never told me he'd changed because of something that happened to you."

"Are you saying that Markus was a Dom just like you and he threw it away to be with me?"

"That's exactly what I'm saying. He wouldn't even introduce you to me for fear you might figure it out. At the time, I thought he was just ashamed of me or something. Now I realize he was trying to protect you from getting hurt again."

"He hid it well," Brianna said sadly. "He was always in complete control in the courtroom, it was so easy for me to see him being in control at home, too. But he turned it off as soon as he walked in the door. I don't understand how he could turn his back on such a big part of who he is."

Lukus finally removed his arm from over his eyes and rolled to his side, resting his head in his hand to hover over Brianna. "It's easy. He loves you more than he loves himself."

Brianna's breath caught. She finally asked the

question he'd been dreading. "Is he ever gonna be able to forgive me?"

Lukus considered her question. "I honestly don't know, sweetheart. You really ripped his heart out and handed it to him on a platter. I've known him for a long time, but I just don't know how this is gonna play out."

"Will you please talk to him for me? Try to explain it to him? I know he won't listen to me, but maybe he'll listen to you." He could see the hope in her brown eyes.

"What makes you think I even want to help you sort this out with him? You made your bed. Maybe part of your punishment is to let you lie in it now."

"I don't believe you. You can't fool me, Lukus. You care about Markus and I think you care about me. Please... won't you at least try?"

It took him a minute to reply. "Shit... I think I'm fucked."

Brianna rewarded him with a killer smile that told him for a fact he was indeed fucked.

*Maybe **my** new nickname should be Mr. Rogers.*

Deciding it was time to reassert himself, Lukus rolled over to the edge of the bed and reached into his nightstand to withdraw a length of rope. He felt a pang of regret at the excitement he saw in Brianna's eyes. On a different day, with a different woman, he could have had so much fun. But not today.

"What's that for?" she asked warily.

"I have a few errands to run and there's no way

I'm giving you free rein over my loft. I should be locking you in the stockade down in the dungeon right about now and then lighting up your ass again with my belt." He smiled a wry smile. "Instead, I've decided that tying you down here to take a nap while I'm gone is gonna have to be good enough."

She grinned. "You'd better be careful, Lukus. If the club finds out you punished me with a nap, it could ruin your entire reputation." Brianna barely got a short giggle out before he flipped her onto her tummy, smacking her ass for good measure. Lukus made quick work of securing both of her wrists to his headboard while she struggled feebly against the rope.

"I can see I've let you get away with entirely too much lip, little girl. Now that you've pointed out the shortcomings in my punishment plan, I'll make a few additions to the agenda before I leave." Once she was secure, Lukus reached back to his private stock of sex toys to grab more rope. Brianna was straining to see, an anxious expression on her face. He flipped her onto her back, reaching to squeeze one of her heavy breasts before getting to work.

"This is called Shibari—more specifically, I'm restraining you with a Bikini Harness." Lukus worked at wrapping the rope around artfully for a few minutes before adding, "It shouldn't be painful. I'm making it just tight enough to act as a constant reminder that you're still being punished while I'm gone."

Just as he finished the wrap, Brianna released an unadulterated groan that sounded much more like pleasure than pain.

You're supposed to be punishing her, not pleasuring her, sport. She needs a Dom. You know what you need to do.

Bri had closed her eyes. She didn't even resist when Lukus rolled her back onto her tummy, her arms stretched up to the headboard. His eyes drifted over the marks Jake had left behind. She may have enjoyed them, but she hadn't consented, and he wouldn't make that same mistake.

"You understand you're being punished, right?"

"Yes."

"Then, if you consent, I'm going to stripe your ass so you have something to think about while I'm gone."

"You're asking me?" Bri lifted her head, turning to look up at him, her eyebrows crinkled as she questioned him.

"I am, considering the circumstances. So... do you consent?" He pressed her.

She hesitated before adding a soft, "Okay."

"Okay, what?"

She paused again before answering perfectly. "Okay, sir. I consent."

He grasped his belt buckle, pulling the wide, well-worn leather free of its confining loops. Brianna couldn't see what was about to happen as he folded the length in half, turning it into one of his favorite implements. He knew it was time to teach her what it meant to be a submissive.

The loud snap of his belt smacking both of her ass cheeks with full force caused his hardening tool to throb. The throbbing got worse as she began calling out his name. He couldn't stop. Instead, he set a steady pace, never diminishing the force of the blows. Within minutes, Brianna was calling out from the blistering pain, but her cries were soon turning to moans of pleasure. That was what Lukus had been waiting for.

He stopped the belting and threaded the belt back through the loops of his jeans. He smiled with satisfaction as he saw his restrained captive writhing on the bed, horny and desperate for release... just like him.

"It seems you need a few lessons on being a submissive, sweetheart, since it's clear you've had no proper *tutor* to date. Lesson number one: You will never again allow yourself to come during a punishment spanking. You don't get to come until the punishment is over and your Master gives you permission. Lesson number two: You will never rub your ass after a punishment. That's just insulting to your Master. If he paddles or whips you as a punishment, it should damn well hurt and for a long time. Nothing pisses me off more than when Masters bring their subs here and I spend time disciplining them only to have their Doms rub lotion on their bottoms. I want you to lay here, horny as hell with your ass on fire. Think about what you did to your husband. Think about just how sorry you really are, like a good little submissive."

He gave her ass one final slap with his palm before pulling the sheet up to keep her from getting chilled. He hesitated for a second before leaning down to quickly kiss the back of her head, taking a deep breath, enjoying the scent of her long hair. He knew it was silly, but he doubted he'd have many more chances to touch his best friend's wife after today.

Brianna was able to roll to her side in spite of the ropes stretching her arms above her head. Lukus could see her watching him as he grabbed a fresh T-shirt from his dresser drawer and pulled it over his head. He stooped to grab his boots from the floor and then turned to give her one last look before he headed out of the bedroom without another word.

Before he reached the elevator, Lukus was already dialing a number on his cell phone. He decided to leave a message when it rolled to voicemail. "Markus, it's me. We need to talk...*now*. I'm on my way to you. You'd better get in the shower and sober up, because I'm in no mood for any shit. I'll see you soon." Hanging up, Lukus grabbed his car keys and wallet from the table near the elevator before heading down to his garage.

Yep. I am so fucked.

The End
To Be Continued in Book Two, **Securing it All**
Release Date ∼ September 1, 2020 - available now on
Amazon

BLURB For *Securing it All* - Book Two

**Punishing his wife for her mistakes was the right choice.
Having his best friend handle it definitely wasn't.**

Choosing dominance should be easy.
He did it for years, and there's too much on the line to fail now.
But Markus has been torn apart by betrayal, twisted up and confused by all the lies.

His and hers. A matching set.

But leaving Brianna at The Punishment Pit didn't help.

Lukus has always been the Master's Master.
Permanent bachelor and hardcore dom, yet seeing Brianna's submission has him wanting more.

But she's forbidden fruit, his best friend's wife, and a good man would help them fix this mess.

Everything is a gamble. A game of pain and pleasure. One that might be too dangerous with all of their futures are at risk.

Warning: ***Securing it All*** is book two in the binge-worthy ***Punishment Pit*** series. This book has naughty BDSM punishments, angsty emotion, second chance romance, and old friendships put to the test. Can you handle it?

Here's a little taste of Securing it All:

Lukus

Lukus's BMW hugged the exit ramp from the expressway at close to double the posted speed. He'd decided to take his pent-up sexual frustration out on his car and was grateful the Saturday afternoon traffic was light. In his condition, if the traffic were any heavier, someone could end up hurt.

He'd never been to Markus's house out in the suburbs, and the anger he'd suppressed for three years was beginning to resurface with each passing mile. It was bad enough that Markus had never invited him over. No. His best friend actually had the balls to request someone else come out from Lukus's company to install the security system during construction of the multi-million-dollar home. By the time it was finished, Markus had married Brianna. Lukus hadn't even been invited to the wedding.

My invitation must have been lost in the mail.

Thinking back to his friend's marriage didn't improve Lukus's mood. Markus had all but dropped Lukus once Brianna had entered his life. Lukus had gone to see Markus at his office one evening after the couple had gotten back from their honeymoon, hoping for an explanation. He'd been moderately drunk. Words had been exchanged and punches thrown. After that, the men had gone nearly a year without speaking.

Only Lukus's arrest over a year ago had brought them back together again. Markus had really come through for him when the chips were down, and while his friend had insisted on keeping Lukus hidden from his wife, he'd just been relieved to resume their friendship. The men had lunch together at least once a week and texted even more frequently. The friends had come to an unspoken truce, agreeing to avoid the subject of Brianna, and why Markus walked away from the BDSM lifestyle.

And now, the last twenty-four hours had pretty much torn down all of the walls holding Markus's secrets at bay. While Brianna had answered some of the questions that had been gnawing at Lukus for years, the knowledge didn't alleviate Lukus's anger. He understood that Markus only sought to protect Brianna from the memory of the abuse she'd experienced, but did he somehow think that Lukus was anything like the bastard who'd abused his wife?

What the fuck did he think I was going to do? Show up at the wedding in leather, whip in hand, and scare the shit out of her?

Lukus wasn't sure what he was going to find when he got to his friend's house. He also didn't have a clue how he was going to look Markus in the eye given his magnetic attraction to Brianna. Just thinking of her tied naked in his bed with her pink, striped ass and bound breasts still had his cock throbbing with desire.

Maybe Markus was right to keep her away from me after all. If I was back at my loft, I'd probably be fucking her silly by now.

Thankfully, he'd had enough willpower to get the hell out of there before he did something stupid. Just thinking of her again reminded him to make a call he'd meant to make as soon as he got on the road.

He dialed Derek. His friend answered quickly.

"Hey," his partner asked. "How's the training going? Did she sign the divorce papers yet?"

Lukus should have been prepared for the question. "No... not yet and honestly, I don't think she's going to. I'm on my way out to talk to Markus about it now. That's why I'm calling. What's Rachel up to this morning?"

Derek laughed. "Well, right this minute she's kneeling under the desk at the office sucking me off. Why?"

"We've discussed this, man. You need to stop bringing her into the security office to service you. All it does is get the rest of the crew all horny and jumpy. Unless you plan to start sharing her, you need to cut that shit out."

"Hey, it's Saturday and I already sent the guys working today out on their assignments. No one is around right now and even if they come back, she can just stay hidden at my feet under the desk."

"Fine, but as soon as you're done defiling your wife's throat, I need you to send Rachel up to my loft to babysit."

Derek chuckled. "What? Did you have some chick show up with a kid she's trying to saddle you with?"

"Don't be an ass. I left Brianna tied up to my bed. She gets upset when she's left locked up. She's terrified of being stuck in case the building catches on fire or some bullshit like that. Honestly, at first I laughed it off, but when I really think about it, I realize we might be putting the submissives in danger when we tie them up and leave them unattended. You think you could send Rachel up to sit with her until I get back?" There was silence on the phone for a few long seconds. "Derek.... you still there?"

"Let me get this straight. You, Master Lukus Mitchell, the hard-ass owner of The Punishment Pit, not only took a sub that you were charged with punishing up to your private loft, but you have her tied to your soft, king-size bed. And now you want my sub... my *wife*... to go keep her company so she doesn't get scared. Is that really what you're saying here?"

"I told you... You know what? Fuck it. I'm sorry I called." Lukus was suddenly self-conscious. Calling Derek seemed like a fine idea before, but now hearing his words coming back at him from his second in command, he sounded exactly like one of the lightweight Doms that he and Derek liked to make fun of—the ones that brought their subs into the club because they were too soft to actually discipline them properly themselves.

Lukus could hear muffled sounds at the other end of the connection. He then heard Derek telling Rachel to go kneel out in the reception area and wait for him. After a few seconds, Derek was back on the line and Lukus could hear the concern in his voice.

"Alright man. What the hell is going on with you? Please tell me you didn't fuck her."

Lukus wanted to be pissed at his friend for even thinking it, but he knew he'd be a complete hypocrite if he busted Derek's balls over his accusation since it had taken all his restraint not to claim Brianna. He took a deep breath and sighed before answering truthfully. "No, man. I didn't fuck her. But I'll tell you... I wanted to... *bad*. I had to get the hell out of there before I did something stupid."

"Shit. Well, yes. Fucking Markus's wife would have been colossally stupid. She's hot, but she's so off limits."

"Tell me something I don't already know. Listen, will you please send Rachel up? I don't want her to even know Rachel is there and under no circumstances do I want Rachel talking to her. Do you hear me? Bri knows next to nothing about Markus in his Dom days and I don't need Rachel filling her in yet. Got that?"

"Sure, I can send her up and she'll do what I tell her. You know that. I'm worried about you though. This isn't like you at all. I hear it in your voice, Lukus. You're getting emotionally invested in this."

"Well, fuck yeah. How the hell can I not after the history Markus and I have had since he met Brianna? There's a part of me that's relieved he's turning to me to help him... like the old days. Then there's a part of me that's furious that I wasn't good enough to be part of their lives before this. He waits until some asshole fucks her and now she's suddenly my problem? But the biggest part of me is pissed because he's trying to throw away something that he should have been taking better care of. Maybe if he'd communicated more with his wife, she never would have felt the need to cheat on him or gotten wrapped up in this sociopath's shit."

"Fuck a duck. You're actually taking her side in

this? She must be part witch to have cast a spell on you and get you this twisted up so fast, man."

"I never said I'm taking her side, dammit. I just spent a few minutes doing something Markus should have done a long time ago. It took me all of ten minutes to figure out what the hell is going on. He was either blind or just didn't give a shit to have missed all of the signs of what she needed to be happy."

"And just what is that, Dr. Mitchell?"

"Screw you, man. I'm sorry I called."

"Okay... I'm sorry. I'll back off. I'll send Rachel up and we can talk about all of this shit later when you get back here. Good luck, Lukus. I don't envy you."

"Thanks. I'll call you later when I'm on my way back into the city."

"Later."

Lukus glanced at his GPS to see how much farther he had to go. He was getting close now and decided to call and let Markus know to let him in.

When the phone rang six times and rolled to voicemail, Lukus lost his temper. "Markus, you'd better be up, sober, and ready to listen. I'm almost there. We have a lot to talk about." He cut the call off.

Within five minutes, Lukus was parking in the brick driveway of his friend's mansion. The early spring flowers were just emerging in the landscaped beds lining the wide walkway to the massive front door. Lukus rang the doorbell several times but got no response from inside. He of course tested the door, but it was locked as expected. After knocking on several doors and windows and phoning Markus's cell phone two more times, Lukus was starting to get worried.

Surely he didn't do something stupid.

Before meeting Brianna, Lukus would have been furious at just the thought of his friend harming himself over a woman. But now, having met Brianna, having held her... hell, he could almost understand the temptation... *almost.*

The next call he made was back to Derek. "Hey man. I need your help. I'm at Markus's house and he's not answering. The house is buttoned up tight, but I need to get in. Can you turn off the alarm from the remote access system and even send a command to unlock the front door?"

"Sure... hold on. You don't think he did something, do you?"

Lukus wasn't about to tell Derek the thought had already crossed his mind. "Naw. I'm sure he just drank like a fiend and passed out. I'll probably need to throw his ass into a cold shower to get him sobered up enough to even talk to him."

After a few minutes, Derek was back on the line. "Okay, you should be able to get in now without an issue."

"I'm going in." Lukus tentatively opened the front door, holding his breath in case the alarm sounded. He was relieved when it didn't. "Thanks, man. I'll call you later."

Lukus quietly closed the door, taking a few seconds to glance around the Italian marble tile of the foyer with the grand circular staircase leading up to the second floor. The floor plan was open and he could see all the way through to the back of the house. The whole great room sported two stories of huge windows that looked out onto a fairway of the connecting country club's manicured golf course. It was the kind of elegant home he'd expected, yet he pushed down his anger that he'd never been welcome there before.

Loud rock music blared throughout the house and Lukus called out, trying to project his voice over the noise. "Markus, where the hell are you?"

As he moved into the great room, he had to step over several broken vases, picture frames, and even a chair that was now in multiple pieces. The mirror over the stone fireplace was shattered.

Lukus finally found Markus sprawled face down on the couch, his left arm hanging over the side. An empty rock glass was discarded nearby. Lukus walked over and gave his friend a poke. "Hey, man. I've been calling you. Wake up. We need to talk."

Nothing.

Time stood still as Lukus waited, holding his breath. Was he breathing? It scared the shit out of him that for the briefest of seconds he actually thought of comforting Brianna through losing her husband. Luckily, self-disgust shoved the vision aside, knowing he'd be lost without Markus, the man he thought of like a brother, in his life.

Don't be a pussy, Mitchell. Reach out and check his pulse.

To Be Continued in Book Two, ***Securing it All***
Release Date ~ September 1, 2020 - available now on Amazon

ABOUT THE AUTHOR

USA Today Bestselling Author Livia Grant lives in Chicago with her husband and furry rescue dog named Max. She is fortunate to have been able to travel extensively and as much as she loves to visit places around the globe, the Midwest and its changing seasons will always be home. Livia's readers appreciate her riveting stories filled with deep, character driven plots, often spiced with elements of BDSM.

- Livia's Website: http://www.liviagrant.com/
- Join Livia's Facebook Group: The Passion Vault
- Facebook Author Page to Like: https://www.facebook.com/pages/Livia-Grant/877459968945358
- Goodreads: https://www.goodreads.com/author/show/8474605.Livia_Grant
- BookBub: https://www.bookbub.com/profile/livia-grant

Connect to Livia's books through her website here.

Black Light Series

Infamous Love, A Black Light Prequel

Black Light: Rocked

Black Light: Valentine Roulette

Black Light: Rescued

Black Light: Roulette Redux

Complicated Love

Black Light: Celebrity Roulette

Black Light: Purged

Black Light: Scandalized

Black Light: Roulette War

Black Light: The Beginning

Black Light: Rolled - coming September, 2020

Punishment Pit Series

Wanting it All - Release 8/18/20

Securing it All - Release 9/1/20

Having it All - Release 9/22/20

Balancing it All - Release 10/6/20

Defending it All - Release 10/27/20

Protecting it All - Release 11/17/20

Expecting it All - Release 12/1/20

Stand Alone Books

Blessed Betrayal

Royalty, American Style

Alpha's Capture (as Livia Bourne)

Blinding Salvation (as Livia Bourne)

Don't miss Livia's next book!

Sign-up for Livia's Newsletter

Follow Livia on BookBub

BLACK COLLAR PRESS

Black Collar Press is a small publishing house started by authors Livia Grant and Jennifer Bene in late 2016. The purpose was simple - to create a place where the erotic, kinky, and exciting worlds they love to explore could thrive and be joined by other like-minded authors.

If this is something that interests you, please go to the Black Collar Press website and read through the FAQs. If your questions are not answered there, please contact us directly at: blackcollarpress@gmail.com

WHERE TO FIND BLACK COLLAR PRESS:

- Website: http://www. blackcollarpress.com/
- Facebook: https://www. facebook.com/blackcollarpress/

- Twitter: https:// twitter.com/BlackCollarPres
- Black Light East and West may be fictitious, but you can now join our very real Facebook Group for Black Light Fans - Black Light Central

Made in the USA
Columbia, SC
08 February 2021